COLD WATER

Gwendoline Riley was born in 1979.

Gwendoline Riley

COLD WATER

_V_

VINTAGE

Published by Vintage 2003

2 4 6 8 10 9 7 5 3 1

Copyright © Gwendoline Riley 2002

First published in Great Britain in 2002 by
Jonathan Cape

Vintage
Random House, 20 Vauxhall Bridge Road,
London SW1V 2SA

Random House Australia (Pty) Limited
20 Alfred Street, Milsons Point, Sydney
New South Wales 2061, Australia

Random House New Zealand Limited
18 Poland Road, Glenfield,
Auckland 10, New Zealand

Random House (Pty) Limited
Endulini, 5A Jubilee Road, Parktown 2193,
South Africa

The Random House Group Limited Reg. No. 954009
www.randomhouse.co.uk

A CIP catalogue record for this book
is available from the British Library

ISBN 0 09 943715 5

Papers used by Random House are natural, recyclable products made from wood grown in sustainable forests. The manufacturing processes conform to the environmental regulations of the country of origin

Printed and bound in Great Britain by
Cox & Wyman Limited, Reading, Berkshire

for my mum

and for Kelly Griffiths and Emma Unsworth

COLD WATER

1

This is a dive bar in the American style. There's worn out red velveteen on the stools, the tables are battered dark wood and dusty artificial ferns froth in long brass planters between the booths. The limited light glows from yellowed glass lamps shaped like clam shells, studded around the grey-green walls. I like working here, mostly: sleeping in the daytime and living the days in the nights; meeting people and listening to stories, while the blue spotlights swim over the banks of bottles behind me. It's never busy until late on, so after I've filled the fridges I do the cryptic crossword in the paper or read, under-lining passages that strike me and Biroing rigid swirls and spoked stars in the margins of my book. I was reading *Death in Venice*, held open by a glass ashtray still hot from the sink, when I first saw Tony, this summer. He grinned at me, pulling on a skinny roll-up, his face burnished by the flare from his lighter and his dipped eyelashes casting a dark shadow, and I had cause to remember a line: '*You mustn't smile like that! One mustn't, do you hear, mustn't smile like that at anyone.*'

He shouldn't have.

The reason I'm here is Margi, who was always working when I started coming down here regularly two years ago. The way she used to stand pulling at her rat's tail black hair, the way she widened her grey eyes at the customers' mildest anecdotes, seemed to me to signal a wild disingenuousness which I could only admire. I studied her from my side of the bar and was in thrall. I asked for a job. She's twenty, same age as me, but a lot, lot wiser I think. I think. She's been wearing the same clothes, more or less, since we met, with maybe a half inch of pale, inner-city midriff visible below a small black T-shirt, above grey, men's trousers which hang off the gentle jut of her hipbones and trail raggedy at the hem, a black tidemark an inch or so up where they've dragged through Manchester's sad, silty puddles.

Customers come and go. The only one who's been here all this time is Kevin Kinsella. I've never really worked Kevin out. I know I don't like the way he sniggers. Don't like how he holds out his beaker and says, 'Can you put another little guy from the top shelf in there please, Carmel.' It winds me up. His bald head is marked with pewtery dents, and his leftover hair is dark blond and fried-looking. He always wears a Hawaiian shirt and a trench coat. He wears two watches, one on each wrist. Neither of them has any hands. I'm not sure what that signifies. On one scrawny forearm is an ancient tattoo of a sea horse, blue-green, the outline indistinct. I can imagine him waiting backstage with a damp bouquet for a pretty redheaded chorus girl. A doll. Staring at his shoes, blushing. Sometimes I think this bar is full of delusionals. Infants. I find it a little sinister. A friend of a friend went round to Kevin's house once and claimed Kevin showed him this video of two Japanese women in a bath, being sick into each other's mouths. I argued about this with Margi a few weeks ago. She said, 'Kev's just like you or me, he's just got his own bubble, his own things that he's into – Bukowski, Damon Runyon, John Fante, all that hard-boiled stuff, and mermaids and whisky . . .'

'And Japanese women being sick in each other's mouths,' I said. 'Where does that fit?'

At this point I picked up one of the coffee cups from the top of the espresso machine and it slipped and smashed at my feet. Shards of thick white china exploded across the dirty floor. I knelt down and started picking them up. Margi flicked me a look and I flushed.

'Accident,' I said.

Lose your temper and lose the fight. That's a life rule, but it's hard to keep to. I'm pretty temperamental, despite myself. Like the time I was pissed off with Tony for going home early without me when I was working. I took a break and sat outside on the ledge in front of the bar with a drink. I got mad when I thought about it and threw my glass into the gutter. It's not good behaviour. It's not very dignified. I thought Tony was long gone, but he'd heard the smash and ran back around the corner in case there was trouble. I don't like to think about the way he looked at me. I went down in his esti-mation right then. I saw it happen in front of my eyes.

I walked all the way back to my flat after work that night, down past the museum and the park. Summer rain fell fast and the leaves dripped. The warm air tasted of mulch and rot. On the edge of town there's a building site where they're putting up a new leisure complex. The diggers were still, poised. To one side huge concrete slabs, dark grey with absorbed rain, were stacked ready to be slotted into place. For a long time I stared down at the churned, live earth, planted with rusted iron bars. In the squat office block behind, a window was broken and the wind was shuffling the grubby vertical blinds, whipping them off the rail.

2

My dad died when I was fourteen. I found him, sitting stiffly on the settee when I came in late one night, his eyes open behind his glasses, and a full ashtray balanced on the arm of the chair. I clicked off the hissing TV and sat down next to him. I wasn't upset. I felt relieved. For us and for him.

My brother Frank and my mum and I moved soon afterwards, from our small semi in Prestwich to a small semi in Whitefield. It was a miserable place, always a mess. There were newspapers and clothes all over the living room floor; picking a path to the settee you would crack Biros underfoot. Tea-stained mugs and dirty plates crowded on the coffee table and the windowsill. My mum pushed the furniture around to cover a carpet filthy with kicked over drinks and thrown food. She was always saying she could never have people round because of the state of the place.

'Like who?' I'd ask.

'Friends.'

'What friends?'

And then there'd be tears. More specifically, there'd be sniffing. I couldn't stand it. All of her crying sounded like singing to me. I thought cruel thoughts like maybe my dad had smacked her in the head once too often. She acted frightened all the time. And there was a petulance in there too, a martyrdom, that's what I couldn't take.

Well, a friend did come round, once, just after we'd moved. An old friend. She turned up unannounced on a Sunday afternoon. Frank was out as usual and Mum and I were sitting watching TV. Mum answered the door in her washed-out blue dressing gown.

She made three cups of coffee and brought them in on a tray with half a packet of Digestives. There was no space on the table so she put the tray down on the floor. This woman, Sandie? Liz?, she perched on the edge of her armchair and sipped her instant coffee with half-masked distaste, delivering a limpid résumé of her life's work, and saying she'd never liked places that were 'touch-me-not tidy'. Mum barely raised her eyebrows and I sat at one end of the settee, with a lazy look on my face. We were united in a sort of grim exhibitionism. I thought so. That woman left and nothing more was said, until the next

9

evening. I rang Mum at work and she had a go at me about it. Said I'd humiliated her. Said she'd been crying in the office all day. When I put the phone down, I sat still for seconds before standing up and going into my bedroom, tearing the mirrored door off my wardrobe, and launching it down the stairs. It rolled on its corners and though it didn't break, it did hit our glass front door and crack that. I kicked the banisters as I walked downstairs. The last one broke, snapping into a static, splintering explosion. I felt a slump of regret. I went outside to wait for Mum to get back, pushing the ice-cold door open carefully so as not to spill broken glass on the step. I closed it behind me. In the moonlight the cracks glittered like a spider's web across the doorway. I sat down on the pavement and shivered.

It was freezing cold but there were still some boys out playing football further up the road, and a clutch of girls waiting at the bus stop. There was litter in the gutter and raggedy dandelions grew tall in the cracks in the smashed kerbstones. I pressed the heels of my hands into the kerb, till the grit imprinted on my palms.

I talked to Tony about all of this. He had a whole different approach to family strife. When his dad kicked off he used to go and sit out in the shed.

He said, 'That was my kingdom when I was growing up. I had an extension lead and a black and white telly, an armchair. Just sat in there smoking and thinking.'

That was Tony all over, I didn't get tired of it. I acted soppy around him. If you can imagine that. If it doesn't sound too grotesque. I was unabashed. I told him he was like a conspiracy with a dream. I told him he was so good-looking it was like GBH. It was hopelessly true. One time we were lying in his bed, our legs were tangled up and he had his arms around me as well. He asked me if I was comfortable and I said yeah and he said good and then I said 'When you've got your arms round me I don't care about anything else in the world'. I half regretted saying it. But he said 'That's good to hear,' and held me tighter and I didn't feel so stupid. He lived in a small flat in Levenshulme. He didn't have a bedside light, he used to pick one of his shirts up off the floor and hang it over the wicker lampshade so it wasn't so bright.

I remember the first time he did that.

★

Outside the bar there's a small wooden cabinet fixed to the wall, on the left of the door. And behind the dust-streaked glass there are a half dozen old photos of the place. Over the years they've faded to an odd aquamarine tint. The long gone barmaids who are smiling shyly for the camera have yellow teeth and greenish skin. There's a snack menu drawing pinned up in there as well, although we've not done food for years.

For a few months at the beginning of the year this scrawny old sod started rolling in late every night. He wore his trousers belted high up over his ribs. His eyes crinkled at the corners when he smiled, although a lot of the time he wasn't really smiling, the shutters were down. Other customers bought him drinks and he held forth. One time he was leaning on the old food hatch at two in the morning shouting 'Cancel the cheeseburger!' I wasn't hurrying to chase him out but Bob the doorman took him by the elbow, respectfully, and led him up the stairs. When he came back down he was shaking his head and frowning. That guy was a snooker world champion years ago so he said, and something of a maverick hero too. Now he hangs around a club in Cheetham Hill, sleeps on the benches there, plays for beer money.

That's okay, I suppose. What I don't like is when these people need to make others complicit in their big lie. When they need an audience to bore or someone to push around. I can't fathom the audacity of that recruitment drive. How can you square that? My dad had my mum trapped in his failing personality, in those four walls. Walls and floors. My mum curled up on the floor.

Still, *any* relationship configures people anew and it's rarely healthy. People don't often touch you like they really want to know you. These days I try to keep everything remote as a matter of course. Just feel the warm rush of things washing over.

★

Tony finished with me at the beginning of September. He sat on the edge of his bed and scratched the back of his neck and stared at the floor and I knew what was coming. Amongst other things he said, 'You don't seem like the happiest of people ... I'm finding it a bit draining, to be honest.'

I didn't know what to say to that. I just said oh right. Didn't ask anything else or cry or enter into a discussion. That's rule number one. I went back to my flat, got drunk there, and then went into work. The bus's reflection slid over the restaurant windows in Rusholme and I saw myself, sitting stationary and ridiculous. I wanted to disappear, to dissolve.

At work, I leant inertly on the bar and wandered among the empty tables. I sank against the back wall and held out my arms. I had a vision of myself as a drowning person. My life stretched out behind me. My hands made stars in the warm blue light.

Kevin was in, as usual. At the end of the night I was stacking glasses in one hand and collecting bottles in the other, slipped into splayed fingers so they hung like bowling pins.

Kevin said, 'I saw you adopting the position earlier, Carmel.'

I smiled as he put his elbows on the bar and held his head in his hands. A familiar posture.

'I was thinking of asking you to hang out with me some time.'

*

So, I arranged to meet Kevin the next Monday, my night off. I really didn't have anything better to do. We met on the steps of Central Library.

Kevin was a little late, ambling up Mosley Street with the collar turned up on his private dick mac and a scattering of raindrops balanced unbroken on his strange yellow hair. It was getting cold, but I didn't mind that he was late. I was in a pretty good mood, all things considered.

'Hey there, Carmel,' he said, with one eye squinted up.

'Hey there, Kevin,' I said. 'Where shall we go then?'

On icy Manchester evenings I like to *stride*, to thrust my hands deep into my jeans pockets and exhale towards the stars, blowing out streams of white smoke; Kevin just sloped along like a teenager, and that irritated me. I had to stop and wait for him to catch up with me, stamping my feet to keep warm. We walked down to Dôme Bar, one of Kevin's other haunts, clean and brightly lit, with a dark wood floor, framed Art Nouveau posters on the bare brick walls and bar snack menus printed in gold script on pale pink card. The barmaids are usually foreign students, Spanish or Italian, and they have to wear crisp white shirts and little half aprons around their waists for the change. They don't lean listlessly against the fridges and gossip together like Margi and I do. They don't read. Occasionally one of them comes round and sits down for a cigarette break, smoking with perfect poise and studied boredom. They have a stereotype to uphold, I suppose. I ordered a Campari and orange, and Kevin had a whisky. We sat on stools at the bar.

'I still haven't found my drink,' I said.

Well, whisky killed my mother so it has semi-romantic associations for me,' he said as he lifted the glass. How drab. Some people carry their emotional life around with them like a dead rat in a shoe box. Ready to whip it open and flash it under people's noses. I felt annoyed with Kevin; he did it with no panache.

I led the conversation because I was in a good mood. I asked him about his day job, which was something in sales, but he didn't have much to say about it. He asked if I was at college and I told him no, I dropped out.

Kevin set up another round. I got drunker and bolder. I said, 'What's with the watches, Kev?'

He stood up clumsily, stuck his arms out at right angles to his body, and said, 'Time-free zone, Carmel!'

The gaps between buttons on his red Hawaiian shirt stretched open, revealing sweaty tufts of ginger hair on his sunken chest. I laughed. He looked uneasy and sat back down, taking a sip from his glass even though it was empty. I bought another round. I'd heard from Margi that he was enquiring into renting a disused Victorian urinal round the back of Piccadilly and turning it into a bookshop. And that he'd been asking all his favourite Manchester barmaids to go and work for him.

'What's with this bookshop then, Kevin?' I said.

He looked embarrassed. He reached up and scratched his bald head. A dark-haired girl came and wiped the bar in front of us. The wood steamed in the wake of the cloth. Kevin cupped his hand around his mouth and whispered, 'I don't know if that's going to happen now.'

'Well, that's a shame,' I said.

I decided to bait him a little, for want of anything better to do.

'But you'd have been selling Bukowski and his lot, wouldn't you? I hate Bukowski. Have you seen that video of him kicking his wife in the face?'

Kevin sighed, 'I don't need to have that conversation.'

And I could kind of respect that. The things you're into are the things you're into after all. A person should be loyal to their obsessions, I think. Kevin changed the subject.

'There's these little kids live a few doors up from me. Kelly and Mark-Anthony Fairclough. Nice kids, always playing out. Recently she's been big into horses, ponies, gymkhana on Sundays all that. In the evenings she brings her saddle out in the street.' Here he paused and took a long swig of his whisky.

'And there's this church opposite, with a low wall out front. She puts the saddle over this low wall and climbs up in it and bobs up and down, pretends she's a lady of the manor.' Kevin imitated this movement on his barstool. 'But the other evening her brother, this Mark-Anthony, who's only tiny, five or six, comes out with the bridle, and climbs over the wall, and puts the bridle *on himself*, then starts galloping around the graveyard giving it all this.' Kevin lifted his hand up behind his head and mimed pulling, lifting his chin up, his eyes bright and cold. He stopped and said, 'You see, he's the horse.'

I nodded. 'Weird kid.'

'Yeah,' said Kevin.

We both upended our drinks and he stood up to go. That bar was overheated and I was glad to feel the stab of cold as I pushed open the door. We walked up through Chinatown. There was a fine rain floating to the ground and the air smelt sweet-rotten from all the bursting bin bags outside the restaurants.

I took a breath and said, 'You know my ex, Tony? He's not like other people. He's from somewhere else and he's going somewhere else. When I first met him I used to think that if I could kiss him just once everything would be absolved. Might sound melodramatic but it's true. I stand by it.'

Kevin was silent for a while, as we walked through the misty rain. Beyond the blackened railway bridges and above the squat buildings, the sky was a wrung grey. I'd mentioned Tony, but he didn't even exist for me anymore. I'd sealed him in the past. He was a myth, he was a rumour, and this talk was just night-time, half-drunk hyperbole. It's really a relief when you can fall out of love. It's one less stone in your satchel. I was concentrating on not treading in the puddles because the water would come up the sides of my Mary Janes and wet my socks.

'Like my wife,' Kevin said. And that surprised me.

I said, 'I didn't know you were married.'

'Well, she's dead now, so I'm not really.' He squinted up one eye and looked at me.

'Oh right,' I said. 'My dad's dead.'

Kevin nodded. Maybe I should have asked about Kevin's wife but I really wasn't that interested. And I was in a *good mood*, like I said.

Kevin and I shook hands at the taxi rank, and as I walked away I had a feeling of sweet relief, of having jettisoned a dead weight.

I was impatient to see Margi. I walked down towards the bar, a way back behind Oxford

Road, past the student bars and the gay village and down a short alley. As I walked, I clenched and unclenched my fists in my pockets. Sometimes to my left or my right I heard the heave-splash of someone being sick. The way was strewn with litter and sodden scree, the walls plastered with posters for club nights and touring bands, which were stained and peeling in ribbons. I smiled at Bob on the door and he raised his eyebrows at me. He looked bored, zipping and unzipping his big black satin bomber jacket. I walked down the steps. The place was empty and Margi was leaning on the bar reading a book. When she heard me come in she looked up automatically and then smiled. She was playing one of her tapes. A reedy male American voice sang a shuffling space lullaby to the empty room:

Baby my head's full of wishes,
Baby my head's full of pictures,
Baby my head's full of colours,
Baby my head's full of pictures of you . . .

The optics have leaked for as long as I've worked here. I watched a sticky stream of brandy wind round Margi's forearm as she pressed a small glass up to the bottle. She'd pulled her hair up into a ponytail, which swept down onto her hunched up shoulders in a straggly S shape. The glass filled up slowly. She put it on the bar and then ducked round to sit next to me. She stretched her skinny forearms out across the bar and laid down her head. The voice sang on,

Baby I spent all my money,
Baby don't think that it's funny . . .

Margi yawned, and kept her eyes closed when she asked me how my night went.

I said, 'Kevin's a nice guy, I'm sure, but his personality is one big short circuit. I couldn't take anymore.'

I took a swig of brandy.

'Yeah?' she said, lifting her head up. 'You may be right. But while we're on the subject, you got a package today, from another one of your admirers. Mackie.'

A package from Mackie. This was great news.

'I thought he'd gone for good,' I said.

'The postcode says Cornwall,' Margi said. 'It's over there. He must be on a cycling tour.'

She put her head back down and giggled into her elbow.

I hopped off my stool, ducked behind the bar

and picked up the small, brown-paper parcel. I unwrapped it carefully. He'd sent me a prayer book. A paled ink stamp told me it was taken from Wesley Church in St Ives and in tiny, slanting green Biro script, in the margin of 'the Apostles' Creed', Mackie had written;

25th September 2000 A.D. To Carmel McKisco, spinster of the parish of Withington, a little souvenir of Alan's Holiday. I went into this church for the harvest service. The church was bedecked with flowers and fruit, with all the ancient Cornish people in flower hats. I have been sitting in hotel lounges watching the sea. All I need is Somerset Maugham to join me for a cup of Earl Grey. I'm listening to Bruce Springsteen — Ghost of Tom Joad. See you soon or maybe not. 'Keep the faith'. From Alan Mackie.

He'd illustrated this missive with strange stilted stickmen, including, as far as I could tell, him and his bicycle on a sinking ship, and me, a smiling mermaid flopping on the harbour wall. I can be sentimental when I'm drunk. And at that moment it meant a lot to me that Mackie had sent me something. Will he ever return I wonder? Or will we just get postcards until the postcards stop?

Margi said, 'Do you want to go to the cinema tomorrow?'

But I'd already decided to go on a day trip the next day. A day trip to Macclesfield.

★

Mackie was always smiling, and that's just one thing I liked about him. He spoke in a high, happy, nervy babble, spraying spittle on the bar. Before I really got to know him, back when he just used to clatter his mountain bike down the stairs and leave it by the cigarette machine while he sipped his one drink – a bottled beer with a glass full of ice – Margi and I used to call him Wet Lips. Soon enough we all got talking, because he was often our only customer when we started our shift.

One evening he produced a notebook with a blue marbled cover. It was stuffed with photographs and scraps of paper. I picked out a picture of a dark-haired girl, smiling in a bottle-green uniform and immaculate straw hat. It was Mackie's daughter, there was no doubt about that. Mackie said, 'That's Stella. She's thirteen now. She lives with Kathleen's mum in Northwich.'

Kathleen was his wife.

'We were like Scott and Zelda,' he'd once said.

'We spun out. We couldn't hold it together.'

. I never asked why.

From what I can gather he was a cross-country cycling champion in his teens, then a marginal figure in the Manchester punk scene, then he joined the navy and when he left he lived in London and busked, and women would drop their phone numbers in his guitar case. He moved to Paris and worked in the British Embassy then came back to Manchester and married Kathleen, an archaeology student, and they went travelling in Egypt. Stella was conceived in Alexandria. 'We *made love*,' he said – Mackie always said 'made love' when describing his romantic encounters – 'We *made love* in a tent.' He also claims to have written the lyrics to The Stone Roses' 'Waterfall'. He was doodling on a postcard in Dry Bar, left it on the table and next thing you know . . .

Margi and I are never sure if he is making these stories up, but we feel inclined to believe him. And anyhow, both Margi and I lie about everything as a matter of course. A line I like from Hemingway is '*I mistrust all frank and simple people, especially when their stories hold together.*' Exactly. I believe in subterfuge. That was something I liked about Tony. He exercised the same technique. Example: he was round at my flat one time, we were lying on my bed listening to records, and for whatever reason I used the word 'obloquy'.

'What's obloquy?' he said.

And I said, 'I'm not going to explain that to someone who uses the word *zephyral* in casual conversation.'

'What's zephyral?'

He closed his eyes and tapped his slim fingers on his belly in time with the music.

'Well you said it, you fuck, *I love Cornwall in the winter, it has a kind of a zephyral beauty*. Quote unquote.'

His grin spread like buttercream. 'No I never.'

And I just watched him for a while. Tony only really admitted to having read one book, *The Grapes of Wrath*. He once said to me, 'That book taught me to chill out and appreciate my life.' That was Tony all over. I think it's quite a beautiful thing to say, although it's not what I got from that book. Not at all. He must have really loved it because he always brought it up when he was a little bit drunk.

I used to run my fingers over the bird bones in his beautiful face, trace my thumb along his eyebrow and then down his jaw. I would tuck his black hair behind his ears. He said, I like it when you play with my hair, it's relaxing. I did it because I never knew what to do. To blush or to bite.

Anyhow, similarly, if people ask, I say I'm a barmaid, not a struggling whatever. I think it's a more dignified way to behave.

Apart from the prayer book, the last time I'd seen or heard from Mackie was at his birthday party, at the end of May. The week previously he'd left an invite for me at work, written on a navy recruitment postcard. Irene, the girl who works the day shifts and manages the place, had propped it up by the Martini. I was 'cordially invited' to the Blackfriars' Arms the next Friday at eight-thirty.

I took the night off work, but went in to see Margi beforehand. Irene was filling the fridges, and Margi was having her break, sitting on a stool at the bar. She'd bought a pomegranate off the Church Street market and was spearing the crimson pips on a safety pin. She looked like Juliet Greco and I told her so. But I'd told her that lots of times before. She said she was getting off work early to see a band at the Roadhouse, did I want to come? And I told her sure, after Mackie's shindig. I had a couple of tequila lemonades before setting off.

It was a warm evening, and I was wearing just a thin blue dress over my jeans and my Mary

Janes, with a twin set cardigan and a hair slide shaped like a seashell. The tall lights in Piccadilly Gardens were casting an eerie medical glow against the smudge-grey sky. I walked slowly down Market Street, which was deserted except for a lone skateboarder, and over the Irwell, pausing to lean over and look down at the grey river.

I lost my way in Salford, amongst the soot-furred bridges and the wide, empty roads. I spotted two red mopeds on the pavement by one of the railway arches. A pizza parlour. I went in for directions. Inside, the brick walls were painted white and at the back a moustachioed chef was illustrated in blinking pink and green neon. A teenage girl stood at the counter behind metal trays and bowls full of cubed ham, sliced peppers, flaked tuna and wet sweetcorn. She wore a grimy white apron over a striped sweatshirt. Her blonde hair was pulled into a high ponytail. The radio played a ballad which I half recognised, but the place still felt silent to me. The one customer was sitting on a slashed vinyl banquette, rolling a cigarette on his knee. I asked the girl about the Blackfriars' Arms and she frowned and said, 'I've not heard of it' then turned and asked this older guy who leant against a tall Coke fridge talking sport with the customer. She had a small constellation of spots on the back of her neck.

I took out the map Mackie had drawn me and pushed it across the counter. SO YOU THINK YOU'RE FIT? it demanded. HAVE YOU GOT THE STRENGTH OF MIND? Alongside the map, Mackie had scrawled in tiny red writing, *'Please go to sea to protect the innocent children of the world.'*

'Let's have a nosy,' the man said.

He knew where I was talking about and I was there in ten minutes. It was so unlit down there, I walked in the very middle of the road.

The Blackfriars' Arms was almost too warm. Convivial is the word for it. There were maybe a half dozen people standing at the small circular bar. I bought myself a gin and tonic. It came in a small wine glass, and the ice cubes were opaque half-moons. Still haven't found my drink. I once read about a cocktail called 'Vieilles Pluies et Poussières' – Old Rain and Dust. I don't know what's in it, but I picture a thin grey syrup with a gossamer rainbow petrol swirl floating on top. Margi and I have tried to mix something appropriate, but it never comes out.

I asked after Mackie. The old lady who'd served me grinned.

'You here for his do, are you? He's in there.'

Picking up my drink, I walked around the

bar to a frosted glass door and pushed it open with my free hand. I had a strange expectation, a half-hope that I might find a room filled with other people Mackie had picked up around the city, in bars and in shops. He did get around on his bike, after all. I'd seen him from the bus several times, swerving around corners, shaking his fist at drivers, and I knew he was a regular at all kinds of places. He'd told me so. I wondered if there might be another barmaid, something like me, sat with Mackie inside. But the small room was empty. No Mackie, even. Although his things were there. On the mantelpiece was arrayed a menagerie of plastic animals. There was also a picture of Shelley Winters and a small bronze model of the Eiffel Tower. Over the small iron radiator he'd hung a white pillowcase on which he'd felt-tipped: '27th Annual Mod Ball' and 'Rule, Britannia, Britannia Rules The Waves'. Two of the tables had been pushed together and covered in blue napkins and there was a bowl of peanuts, a bowl of tortilla chips, a carrot cake decorated with a white fondant '27', a ship in a bottle and a heavy wooden book end carved with gargoyles. Framed photographs were propped on the dado rail: Mackie with fists aloft crossing the finishing line in a bike race, Mackie leaning on the bonnet of a 2CV; Mackie's wedding day; Mackie at the Pyramids. I couldn't help laughing out aloud.

Mackie appeared.

'Carmel! You came! I didn't think you were coming.'

He smiled a wet smile. I gave him a clumsy hug and handed him the card I'd made. He was wearing a shiny silverish suit which was too short in the arm and leg, a black shirt and his baseball cap.

'You're not twenty-seven,' I said, pointing at the cake.

'Yeah, but it's the twenty-seventh today,' he said, and sighed.

'So it is,' I said.

I sat down, stretched out my arms, and put my feet up on a stool. I felt happy and at home. I took a handful of crisps. Mackie sat down next to me, but leapt up again almost instantly to get a picture from across the room. It was one of the pub's, a sepia print of some schoolchildren on Piccadilly way back when.

'Look at all the poor raggedy boys,' he said earnestly and I leant in to look.

Mackie and I chewed the fat. He drank his beers with ice, and I stuck with gin and tonic. We talked about the parties he'd been to in Paris, when society girls arrived with cobras draped round their necks. We talked about his wife and his daughter.

He said, 'Stella's a flower child now. She listens to all Kathleen's old records: The Byrds, Buffalo Springfield. She's a West Coast girl.'

At one point he said, 'I was a beautiful baby, Carmel. All the nurses loved me. My mum says they used to hold me up and say "Hey, where did you come from, blue eyes?"'

I asked him if he was going on holiday in the summer and he said yeah, he always went down to Cornwall.

'You have to see it down there, Carmel, it's like another country. There's different flora and fauna and all the children are like pixies.'

'That sounds great,' I said.

The landlady came in after she'd rung time. She leant on the door frame and smoked a cigarette, picking up her feet one at a time and flexing her toes in her trainers.

'How you doing, love?' she said. 'You can leave all this stuff 'til tomorrow if you need to.'

'This is my friend Carmel,' Mackie said. 'She works across town.'

The old lady laughed.

'Hi there,' I said.

I wonder what I looked like, sitting there. What the hell.

'Thanks for coming, Carmel,' Mackie said, and he smiled.

We walked outside together. Mackie pointed up at a dark high-rise.

'I live at the top. You should see my flat sometime. It's like the British Museum.'

I wanted to ask him something grandiose and sentimental, like *are you happy, Mackie?* But what's the point. It would have been self-indulgent. Mackie unclasped a red enamel badge from the lapel of his jacket and leant in to pin it on to my cardigan. It said 'Belle Vue Aces Supporters' Club'. He nodded at the effect.

'My dad used to take me to the speedway when I was a teenager,' he said, 'and I always wanted to stand on the corner so I could feel the ash fly in my face.'

*

'This is a song about a spider that gets trapped in its own web.'

I recognised the tune from the tapes Margi played in the bar. There was a small crowd in the Roadhouse, mostly standing amongst the black-painted pillars towards the back of the room. I saw Margi as soon as I walked in, dancing alone in front of the speaker stacks. Strands of hair that weren't caught up in her ponytail were stuck with sweat in streaks and whorls on her pale neck, lit by the band's backdrop projection of a blue-grey blistered moonscape. I went up to her and touched the small of her back, and she turned around and smiled. She held both of my hands and she said, 'Dance with me.'

She looked into my eyes with her saucered, unfocusing eyes and she mouthed the words to the song. I felt an old, sad un-connection somewhere in my chest. But I smiled back at her. She spun me around to a strange, stop-start waltz-time, holding both my hands and looking into my eyes the whole time.

'This next one's about being taken by aliens and liking it. It's called "Happy Abductees".'

I let go of Margi's hands but kept dancing. I flickered my fingers in front of my eyes. She did the same. I leant forward and said, 'Where are these from?'

'Stalybridge,' she said and spun around on her heel.

I looked up again at the figure hunched over the microphone singing, dead still except for a few inches of his untrimmed D-string, a glass needle which quivered in the white stage light.

When the band had finished, shuffling off to scattered applause, Margi went to the bar and brought us back a whisky each, no ice, in plastic

tumblers. We sat down on the edge of the stage
to drink them.

'You been to Mackie's birthday party?' she said,
smiling.

'Yeah. There was only me there. Was all right
though. I'll tell you about it another time.'

Margi leant back and lay down and pulled her
feet up onto the stage and I did the same. I liked
it back when she got like that. Even if it was
bad for her. I liked it, that's the truth. I reached
for her hand and looked up into the glaring
spotlights. I didn't move until I felt somebody
touch my shoe, my scuffed Mary Jane. With an
effort I raised myself up on my elbows.

'Hasn't your bike got any brakes?' he said. It
was the guy who'd been singing. He widened
his eyes at me then nudged Margi in the ribs.

'What's your name?'

Margi opened her eyes but didn't speak.

'That's Margi,' I said, and he looked at her and
nodded.

We took him across to the bar in time to catch
Irene before she locked up. She chivvied the last
customers up and out, paid Bob and turned the
main lights off. We all sat round in one of the
booths with more drinks: yellow beer and dark
liqueurs. The table was covered in different
shaped glasses. Margi did most of the talking.

Her teeth were clicking and she was slamming the table with her fist. The guy flicked his lighter on and a buzz of light illuminated his face. He was squinting one eye up at Margi. I yawned and stretched.

'Don't yawn,' Margi said. 'Don't yawn, we're having a party.'

I said, 'I'm not yawning, I'm cheering silently.'

Three weeks later and they were living together, Margi and that singer, Gene O'Brien. He moved into her flat in Longsight. Some record company was about to sign him, but when the crucial call came, the way Margi told it, he just said, 'My beans are burning,' and put the phone down. He often didn't move from the settee for days, lost in endless, addictive daydreams, watching videos of the moon landings. Margi didn't mind. I remember her smiling and saying,

'I told him, you could have gone to Cape Canaveral with that money, but he wouldn't have. What he has done is bought this grey jumpsuit and all these iron-on fabric patches, First Officer etcetera. He's started wearing it around the house.'

3

It's wonderful to wake up with a project in mind; to leave the house with a mission. I set off for Macclesfield wearing my dustbowl jeans, a red jumper, new socks and my Mary Janes, with my leather jacket and my standard issue black wool Salford bin man hat. I was gleaming with intent, thinking *This is the life!*

I jumped the 9 o'clock London train from Piccadilly, and stood between two carriages so I could see the ticket inspector coming. It smelt of burning dust, the window was streaked with dirty rain and the rubber sealing was snaking itself unstuck from the doors. I had tea in a cardboard cup and an apple. I pulled the window down and felt the biting wind on my face. As the train gathered speed, the scrub on the embankment blurred to a grey-brown brushstroke. I was going to Macclesfield on a strange kind of pilgrimage. Maybe that's the wrong word. I used to go there from time to time, to revisit something, to keep in touch.

A room or a page or a cinema screen – you can take that space and charge it or configure it, give it its own laws and logic, like Orton and Halliwell in their hothouse bedsit room. It's the same when you find a real friend, like Margi or Mackie. Someone puts their arm around you. That seems like the most wonderful thing to me. Human beings are only this size and shape after all. Does that sound terribly bleak and small now I've articulated it? On the train I looked up at the sky all tied up with electric wires and I wanted to wind them all around my fingers.

When I was fourteen I started to go and watch bands, on my own mostly. There was one particular band, they came from Macclesfield, as it so happens. Sometimes when I was watching them, I'd feel my breath pulled out of me, it meant so much. Their songs were simple and direct, about violence, frustration, claustrophobia, *escape*. They never escaped though. That's a judgemental thing to say, isn't it? Maybe I'm missing the point.

I watched the balding ticket inspector hove into view, holding onto the tops of the seats as if he were walking a rope bridge. Some people stuck their tickets out without looking at him, men patted their pockets and women pulled their bags onto their knees to rummage. I ducked into the toilet, locked the door and waited for the Tannoy to tell me I'd arrived.

Macclesfield is a cold and plain town. From the station platform you can survey it, crouched in a small, plain valley; cheap 'Fancy Goods' shops, electricians and chain bars strung along the high street; the town hall up a steep cobbled road, and small grey-yellow stone houses on spokes stretched out behind the shops.

On this occasion I didn't just go into the town centre, but turned back on myself on leaving the station, went under a low flyover, and up a gently sloping residential street. The sky was a luminous white above the craggy hills. I walked for about fifteen minutes, then turned back and walked down on the other side of the road, to a pub I'd seen on the way up. The building was plain, box-like, stuccoed in a cold-porridge fawn colour, the gutters were painted red and the name fixed in plain red letters, the Bridgewater. I went in. It was quiet, just two old guys sat at the bar, both wearing pale jeans and thick cardigans. There was horse racing on the TV, but the volume was down and neither of them was watching. There was a tinny Merseybeat tune on the jukebox. I ordered a brandy and Coke and a bag of crisps from the boy behind the bar, and went and sat in one of the snugs. I stayed in there until mid-afternoon, got half drunk, then walked down to the station.

I was back in Piccadilly by three and decided to stick around in town until work started at six. I went and walked around Kendal's department store. On the ground floor I sprayed some perfume on my scarf. I can't remember what it was called. It was in a red bottle, it smelt heavy, vanilla laced with musk. It cloyed in my throat. The cosmetics counter girls were making me feel flakey and garish. I took the escalator up to Home Furnishings and wandered around, picking up thick towels and sheets wrapped in Cellophane, flicking over the price tags on lamps and vases. I was dimly aware of the piped music and of my footsteps tack-tacking on the vinyl tiles but smothered in the areas of thick carpet. I could smell the perfume on my scarf. I felt agitated. I felt like a loaded gun. But where's a girl to go? Because Manchester isn't Paris; you can't sit out under lime trees. In the first few weeks after Tony I was hardly ever at my flat. In the daytime I went to the cinema, to the library, to the bar. When I was feeling really low, I went to the department stores. I found they focused thought.

After work I often found somewhere else to stay; stumbled up endless tatty staircases – the flowered carpets dissolving to dust in the middle of each step. Sometimes the sun was already coming up, the grey light edging through uncurtained windows. It's not good to be the last person at the party, that's a life rule I know, I know. All the same there were times when I didn't want to go back to my flat after work. I can't say why and I'm not proud of myself.

I remember endless white-walled rooms with their precarious stacks of paperbacks and their record collections, their Blu-Tacked hero galleries and spilling ashtrays. Endless stories. Because everyone's got a story, haven't they?

Here's a sad story. My mum went out with someone called Joe Wilson while she was at university and for six years on and off afterwards. Joseph David Wilson became an almost mythological figure in our household. I know all the anecdotes, all the pet names, their lovers' idiom: when they went to watch a Western he always called it *Ambush at Apache Gulch*. He was her soul mate, a kindred spirit, so she said, and why shouldn't it be true? When they finally split up for good she was so lonely she married my dad on the rebound barely six months later. It happened just like that.

I used to worry about her, and there's nothing worse than worrying about your parents. Now it all seems irrelevant. They're both of them like pieces that have been removed from the game board. Mum used to tell me all sorts of stories. Like when she was in junior school she desperately wanted to go to ballet classes, and on Saturday mornings she used to watch from the bay window in the front room; see all the other girls go by to the church hall, and she asked her mum why she couldn't go but she just sneered at her and said, 'What would you want to do that for?' When she was twelve she went to France for a school trip and outside a café a French boy slipped a note into the hood of her mac; it said *'Miss, you are very lovely'*. She's still got it somewhere; a thin page torn out of a French diary, *'Samedi'*.

And she never stopped thinking about Joe. All those years. He once told her he liked her wearing nail varnish, and in all the photos from when she was first married to my dad, she's wearing nail varnish, and she told me that's because she kept thinking that any day she might bump into him in town. It's a truly *pathetic* detail, isn't it? In the true sense of that word. It used to make me crazy looking at those photos. Dad always seemed to photograph Mum when she was off guard; when she'd just woken up, when she'd just come in from shopping. He thought it was funny. He was trying to get one over on her. That's why they're ugly pictures. I hate my dad. I can't forgive him, even now. I just think of Mum frightened, covered in bruises or all curled up on the floor and I can't stand it. She says she almost stabbed him once, when he was asleep, drunk, on the settee, but she didn't want to go to prison for him. Then he died of his own accord.

I went up to Central Library after school once, and searched through all the phone directories. Sitting cross-legged on the scratchy carpet tiles, I slid the heavy books off the shelf one by one, writing down numbers from all over for J.D. Wilson. I gave them to Mum. I was desperate, desperate for her to find him. Then one weekend, months later, the phone rang, and I answered it. It was a man's voice, gruff, Scouse.

'Hello, is that Linda? This is Joe. Joe Wilson.'

She didn't tell me she'd contacted him.

Frank said, 'She probably didn't let on because you'd get all obsessed and weird over it.'

That hurt. I asked her about it and then she told me she'd written a letter to his parents' old address in Liverpool saying something like, '*With miniskirts back in fashion and Cher back in the charts I thought I'd have my own 60s revival and get in touch with you . . .*' Unbearable pathos. He'd been married and divorced and he'd been living in Canada, of all places. I helped her choose what to wear for their dinner date. She was excited, then, and conspiratorial. I couldn't sleep that night. I sat up in bed, alive to the sound of the traffic, waiting for the slowing sound of one car turning into our road, waiting for a spoke of amber light to swing across my ceiling to show she'd come back.

And the punchline is . . . she didn't like him one bit when they met up. Do you expect me to feel sorry?

★

One of the regulars I've got a lot of time for is a guy called Gareth. He's twenty-nine, a barman in a restaurant across town, and a very intense individual. When he's making a point he jerks his chin to one side; when he's saying something earnest he closes his eyes. He has a great walk and a great vocabulary. He's extremely handsome, with those sleepy eyes and his dark hair in a cowlick quiff. He knows it too. He's a real peacock all told, a windswept peacock, but I don't mind, I'm always pleased when I see him stride in. I leave whoever I'm on with to work alone for a while and lean over the bar to talk to him.

Since it's got cold he's been sporting a pristine white scarf around town. He doesn't take it off when he's inside. He was in here the other week and Irene kept shaking her head and saying, Why's he wearing that in here? I told her, 'Irene, he's not wearing it for *effect*, he's wearing it for *affect*. He's debonair. Is that a crime?'

I got myself a drink and went to talk to him. We discussed summer holidays. It was my topic *du jour*. I asked him about Cornwall. He'd been once.

'It's just full of ex-tin miners who are too drunk to function,' he said.

He didn't see the point of travel.

'Fuck that,' he said, 'you're still the same up here.' He tapped at his temple and flashed his eyes at me.

I leant forward across the bar and said, 'Exactly!'

Well, he was almost right, anyway. Obliquely, he was right. I know I've no desire to swim with dolphins or see the Taj Mahal. I had a fling with Gareth after Tony, and it was much as I might have expected. One time I was lying back on his immaculate bed, and he stared at me for a long time, then he said, 'You're so beautiful it's almost incredible,' with total conviction, and he closed his eyes as he said it.

And I said, 'Oh, Gareth, it's only skin deep.'

He narrowed his eyes. 'But people ruin beauty . . . *so easily*, like just by opening their fucking mouths. Not you though, just gets better I reckon.' He nodded at this, agreeing with himself.

I gave him a hug for that. I like Gareth a lot, he's still my pal. He lives in a garret room in Burnage. In the polystyrene tiles on the sloping ceiling above his bed I noticed dozens and dozens of small depressions where he'd pressed in his fingers.

'Is that what you do all day?' I said to him.

'Yeah,' he said, and reaching up with one hand he started rhythmically pressing his finger in, making a line of little hollows. 'And I did these ones while you were here.'

The word fling is misleading, actually. I was in his bed with him often enough, but I never got undressed, I never kissed him. I didn't feel that way about him. Well, I felt that way about him once, but I didn't do anything about it, damn fool that I am. It was one morning, when he came into the bedroom after his shower wearing just these tiny blue shorts, and then blow-dried his hair in front of his full length mirror while I sat on the edge of his mattress with a cup of tea. I told Irene about that, which isn't really good protocol, but I couldn't resist.

'That's a haunting image, Carmel,' she said.

This time last year I was spending a lot of time with a Czech girl called Katja. She lived in a flat on the third floor of a low-rise in Hulme: a place she used to call Hulme State Pen. I think she maybe had that in mind when she shaved her head. It suited her. She was beautiful enough to carry it off. After she did it people often thought we were together, a couple. I didn't mind that at all.

She grew up in Prague, and came to Manchester five years ago to finish her English degree. She never did, but she thought and dreamt in English, so she said. I've never been to Prague but I've read the books and I can picture a white mist over a river, and wide bridges, and statues of supplicant saints. Katja lived behind all that, however, with her grand-parents, halfway up a high-rise in the scrub.

Her voice was deep and austere, it always made me think of Nico, who also ended up in Manchester, of course, riding round Prestwich on her bike, wearing a long black cape. I never deleted the messages Katja left on my answer-phone because they sounded so strange and beautiful. One time, after we'd had a day out around town I came back to this:

'I'm reading Oscar Wilde, *The Picture of Dorian Gray*. He says *You will always be in love, you will always be in love with love. A grand passion is the privilege of those with nothing to do*. Ding dong.'

Very astute. We had nothing to do. But we had lots to do.

We always arranged to meet outside Central Library. I'd sit waiting on the cold stone steps, with my hat pulled down to cover my ears and my scarf pulled up, to cover my nose. Katja was always late. She would have the names of the books she wanted to look for written in her curious continental handwriting in a small card-covered notebook. She kept this book in the back pocket of her jeans, and its sharp corners had worn out two bullet-shaped holes in the grey denim. After the library we would take our armfuls of books and go to the cinema opposite. We saw every film, even the terrible films, even the children's films.

All through November she worked in the gift shop down at the Lowry Centre. Because she often came and sat at the end of the bar, keeping me company on dead nights, I thought it only right that I should take the tram and see her in work once in a while. I would wait at the platform by the war memorial in St Peter's Square. In the bright winter sun the tram rails stretching down to Salford shone white. The puddles were like silver leaf. I always felt romantic on days like that, with in-between weather. They gave me an electric feeling.

When I got to the Lowry Katja might be sitting at the till flicking through a book of post-cards, or wandering around rearranging the displays; the wicker baskets full of novelty pencil sharpeners and leather bookmarks and rubber lizards and cardboard solar system mobiles. She had to wear a baggy purple shirt and a name badge. I would loiter like a customer until she blinked out of her daydream and smiled and said, How long have you been standing there?

I was hanging out in the shop with her one day, and on her lunch break, instead of us going up to the staff canteen she told me to come with her into the main auditorium.

'You have to see this,' she said.

She pushed open the heavy, silent doors and we slipped into the theatre. The place still had a distinctly new smell: a rubbery, paint and glue and sawdust smell. We sat down on the back row and watched the stage: a ballet rehearsal. There was a man in a T-shirt and grubby tights and legwarmers and a woman in a pink sweatshirt and shorts with her dark hair in a low bun. He lifted her up effortlessly. I lolled my head backwards, and looked up at the lighting rig, and the tier of seating above us, but Katja was concentrating.

'They're so graceful,' she said, her voice low and reverent, 'so beautiful . . . I'm never going to be like that, I can't own that . . .'

I looked at her. I recognised the sentiment. She frowned and then ran a hand over her prickly head and it struck me that she was the most graceful person I'd ever seen.

'You're so continental,' I said. 'You don't have to look like Emmanuelle Béart to be graceful, what a cliché . . .'

She handed in her notice there not long afterwards. She'd got bored with it. I never knew her work anywhere more than six weeks. It was good for me at the time, because it meant she had her days free again.

One morning we decided to walk down to the museum.

'Self-improvement!' Katja said, 'Ha!'

The gutters were thick with slush on Oxford Road, the wind bit. Katja pointed out the rows of institutional windows at St Mary's Hospital because, with the snow in their corners, they looked like a Christmas card.

We went in the natural history room first. Downstairs were the moth-eaten mammals. I pressed my face against the glass cabinets and pulled the same faces as the tigers and the foxes in their curious *mise-en-scènes*. Bared my teeth. Upstairs, on a balcony with an iron balustrade, we lingered amongst the birds on bare branches and the drawers full of pinned insects and dead eggs.

To get to Katja's flat I would walk down past the student halls on the left, and the junkyard on the right; under the flyover and for two minutes along the dual carriageway, where the gutters were filled with broken glass and leaves rotting to black, finally ducking through a hole stretched in low aluminium railings to reach her building.

The light in her stairwell was a sickly yellow green; it was always deathly quiet in there, and all the times I visited I never saw anyone else coming in or going out.

Her routine was simple. On Tuesdays she would collect her dole, and after paying her bills she spent the remainder, which was very little, on books, films, music, magazines. On weekday afternoons she might draw the curtains and watch old films on Channel 4, or bang out poetry on her typewriter. She lived on soup and toast, coffee and biscuits. Something she always used to say was 'I'm full of broken biscuits.' I liked that phrase. I liked the fact that she always had biscuits in the tin, but I confess I found something supercilious about it too. She projected an image of having mastered a system of happiness that relied on the freedom that total poverty afforded her. I found it quite audacious, back then, but I was wrong. I missed the point.

Just before Christmas she decided to decorate her bedroom and I said I'd help out. I've never done anything to my flat, I think it would be a slippery slope, but I liked the idea of making Katja's joint less miserable.

First, we stencilled tiny gold seashells at dado height round the ivory walls, and then Katja pinned up some red velveteen from Arndale Market over the windows, while I Blu-Tacked these paper lanterns we'd bought together in Chinatown to the ceiling. They looked pretty: deep crimson with tiny pink tassels. I stuck fairy lights around her make-up mirror and then stuck up the pictures we'd had enlarged from post-cards - Theda Bara as Salome and Montgomery Clift, reclining in a director's chair, script open on his knee, cigarette. When we'd finished we had a glass of red wine each. When Katja got drunk her cheeks glowed.

'Thanks for being my friend,' she said, without

looking at me, and nodded, and pointed her toes at the gas fire.

Her tights twinkled cheaply in the light of the bluey-orange flames and her face dissolved into the vague dusk. The fairy lights cast weird shadows like barbed wire.

On Tuesday nights we went without fail to this particular bar up Oldham Street. To a night billed as '*Bar Room Blues for Has-Beens, Wannabes, Dreamers, Orphans and Tramps*'. The young DJ played Sinatra, Tom Waits, Nick Cave, Patsy Cline. Katja had photos of all these people pinned up on the cork tiles in her kitchen. Sitting up at the bar, we made our drinks last for hours, chewing the fat with the bar staff. When we tried going to other places she always hated it. Once we were out in a club and she whispered to me, 'Are these people happy?' and I said well, yeah, I think so and she shook her head and said 'It makes me feel empty – empty like a bin bag.' So from then on we tended to just go to this one place, and I began to realise that, outside of work, I didn't like company that much. Her friendship just made me feel freighted.

I called in on Katja one Saturday morning in late December and she wasn't herself. Her grandma had phoned. She glowered from the settee and said, 'Y'know, Carmel, I'm so, so sick of this situation, of everyone asking "And what are you doing now?" Like I'm just converting my latest book for the big screen, and finding a cure for cancer and AIDS. God!'

I felt uneasy at this outburst because she'd never spoken this directly before. I went into her overheated kitchenette to make tea. It was really too hot so I pulled back a corner of the curtain, and leant over the sink to open the window. Through the dirty glass the expanse of new sky in Hulme was a startling, luminous white shouldered by the low swoop of the deserted flyover. Back through the grainy mist, the red neon PALACE sign hung dimly. I let the curtain fall back into place. Katja continued, 'I've got no money to go anywhere, or do anything. I painted myself into a corner . . . I mean, I like it here, for some reason I do. But occasionally I think . . . I don't want to live out the rest of my life in a fucking box in Hulme, y'know? You do know Carmel, don't you, you're the same.'

I was livid. She'd broken a tacit agreement that to me was set in stone. I'll admit, I thought *You're not going anywhere, Katja.* She went on, and she was crying, and her voice wasn't beautiful anymore.

'I've run out of energy. Every morning when I go down to collect my mail, I say to myself, please, please today let there be something in the post that's going to change my life. On every step, *please please please* . . . I'm sorry Carmel, but what do you want me to do? Throw sugar in your face?'

I stopped hanging out with her so much after that. Those were bland words she said to me: 'you understand, you're the same.'

Sometimes I have this desire, this strange desire, for somebody to really tell me, beyond argument and without mercy, exactly *what they know* about *what I am*, to ridicule my clothes, to tear apart my tastes, my pretensions, my sentimentality, to take me by the collar and lay it on the line. I want to *burn* with that truth. It's an idle, narcissistic daydream I have. I've not seen Katja for months and months now.

★

I've heard that under Manchester Cathedral is a Victorian street that has been built over, but is preserved intact. Legend has it there are people down there too. I was riffing about this with Gareth not so long ago. He said, 'Yes it's true, there's smudge-nosed chimney sweeps and girls in mob caps carrying bundles of penny dreadfuls . . .' Here he paused to swig his beer. 'And they're all bloody cockneys for some reason.'

That made me laugh.

4

They're digging up Piccadilly Gardens. Behind a maze of temporary grill fences there are heaps of different coloured rubble: dark brown, red and a light, chalky beige. Small, yellow drill vehicles peck at the pavement and larger diggers scoop out pits. They're making a 'Japanese water park'. I'll believe it when I see it. Margi told me Gene submitted his own plan to Manchester City Council. His proposition was themed around the album covers of his favourite band, Devo, with giant granite spacesuit helmets amid sweeping geometrical manicured lawns and spurting fountains.

I walk past there a couple of times a month when my wages run out and I go down to sell my books at a small shop on Shudehill. I walk down the tram line, past all the grand old Victorian trade buildings with their company names engraved in the sandstone. The Co-operative Insurance Company has its windows boarded with black-painted plywood, and across the way is its new home, a glass low-rise that looks like a stranded spaceship. But all the old rag shops in Smithfield are still clothes whole-salers, with garish disco gear and sequinned jumpers for the middle aged on mannequins in their windows. Along the way there's also the tattoo parlour where Margi and I went when we were having an afternoon on the town. We were like two sailors on shore leave that day. It's a reputable place though it doesn't look it. Shabby pigeons sit fatly on the shrubs which are growing out of the derelict upstairs windows.

The bookshop also sells videos, comics and porn mags. These are all in Cellophane covers, kept in date order in metal shopping baskets on a trestle table. If I see a man looking through them I'm always sure to stare and shake my head and hiss. I can't help myself. There's one guy works there who always gives me a fair amount of money for what I'm selling; another one, the boss I presume, who tends to tut and shake his head and reject everything. I can tell if my preferred bloke is working because there will be triumphal classical music blaring from the small speaker over the doorway and up the road. He's a skinny sort, must be in his late thirties, he has an American army buzzcut and always wears a white shirt and black shiny suit trousers. He's a smirker. He smirks when I walk in, and he smirks as he looks through the things I've brought to sell. I pile my books on top of the counter and he goes through them three or four times. Occasionally he'll pick one up and ask what I thought of it and I'm never sure if I should say it was great to make him buy it, or if he really wants a conversation. I usually leave with about fifteen quid in my pocket, though, which is four films, or two paperbacks, or an album, or two bands at the university or three at the Road-house, or half a night's drinking.

It used to cut me up, selling my books and my records, but increasingly I enjoy having to do it. It makes me feel streamlined. There's very few books I want to keep once I've read them. And how many records does a person need anyhow? I just need a record to put on when I get up, one for when I'm getting ready to go out and one for going to sleep to. Replace them regularly and that's all I need. There's only so many bands that have really meant something to me over the years.

While we're on that subject, here's something that happened to me not long after I started working here. I was sitting at the bar after my shift, drinking my staff drink, a brandy and Coke, and doing the crossword in the paper. The man sat up on the stool next to me had been trying it on all evening. He was in his mid-twenties, with his blond hair crew-cut. He was handsome in a crumpled kind of way: his cheeks were a little rosy, his eyes a little glazed. He was wearing lots of vintage denim, with a paunch visible under his brown T-shirt. I recognised him, but I wasn't letting on. Now he took his chance. 'What are you reading?' he asked. I rolled my eyes. 'I'm Neil,' he said, 'And what's your name'. Then he asked me what kind of music I listened to. I threw out a few names.

'I used to be in a band,' he said. 'Drummer.'

'Yeah,' I said. I turned over the paper and started Biroing in the eyes of a TV personality, 'I know you did.'

'Okay, well what band did I used to be in?'

I told him.

'Yeah! So did you ever come and see us? No, you must be too young.'

'I was fourteen.'

I have a vivid memory of the very first time I saw his band, at a small club in Liverpool, and more particularly of the train journey back. I looked at my reflection in the window and at the houses and high-rises outside, feeling every-thing, *everything*, tauten with a new significance. Everything was charged. The train was full of drunken men, lurching in the aisle, shouting at their girlfriends or any other women who caught their eye. *Christ*, I thought, and I felt for my concert ticket stub in my pocket. I repeated the singer's words in my mind. Steven Unsworth. On stage, he kept his free hand folded up behind him like a wine waiter and it looked awkward, but occasionally he would reach up and grab hold of the collar of his jacket, pull it tight, and when he did that he had sparks coming off him, it seemed to me.

After that gig I saw him standing outside the club helping to load the back line into the van. I didn't say anything. What was there to say? I just stood in the road, looking at him. He rubbed his short, sweaty brown hair about and laughed at something the roadie told him. He was wearing cords and winkle-pickers and a leather jacket and so was I. I realised then that he was a symbol of something important, and I still believe it. There was another girl waiting. She twirled her heel on the Tarmac, dipped her eyelashes and simpered, 'How does it feel to know you're going to make it, Steven?'

He smiled and looked at his shoes. 'Oh, I'm really wiped out right now, that's all I can think of.'

He smiled again, at both of us, and then disappeared into the van.

I put his EP on when I got in, quietly, so I didn't wake Mum or Frank. Before the song kicked in, the thick needle ground into the vinyl, with a sound which always made me picture a beautiful, bored girl, sat up at a bar, Edward Hopper style, draining the last of her drink. I lay down on my bedroom floor, closed my eyes.

This guy started clicking his fingers to get Irene's attention; he offered me a drink, but I said I was fine thanks.

'Course, we've split up for good now,' he said.

'Oh, yeah.'

He swigged his beer. 'The record company got fed up with us I think, especially Steven, of course. Mostly Steven. So now Spencer's back at college, Jack's doing session work, I'm managing some people and as for Steven . . . Steve's still on smack, so . . .'

'Oh really, smack . . .'

'Yeah. Yeah. Living in a squat back in Macc. I haven't seen him in years now. He's totally fucked up.'

I looked him in the eye. 'Oh right.'

He hit his stride. 'You can't help those people . . . you really can't.'

He hopped off his stool and stumbled towards the door at the back. 'I'm just going for a slash.'

I raised my eyebrows at Irene, then reached

over and started looking through the pockets of his jacket, putting keys, money and a dented tobacco tin on the bar, before easing out a scuffed leather address book and flicking through the greasy pages until I found what I was looking for, tore off a corner of my newspaper and copied it down.

★

I always say the world's a better place because of the people who go for long walks. I walk into work a lot in the summer, not so much when it gets really cold. It takes me forty-five minutes if I really march. One evening recently I set off, wearing my navy space cadet dress with black tights and my All Stars. I always forget that one shoe has a hole in the bottom, then I tread in a puddle and feel something like a cold coin in my sock and before too long it gets pretty itchy and uncomfortable.

As is often the case, all of Manchester, all the pavements and the buses and the buildings were slathered in a thin, slippy, silty rain. Everything looked dirty. Everything dripped.

Just past Rusholme I saw Margi's Gene. He was wearing a big grey hat with earflaps and a hefty blue anorak with his jeans, pulling posters out of a record bag and spray-mounting them

62

to the plywood awnings around where they're building a new multi-storey car park.

'Hey there, Gene,' I said, above the ringing drills, 'how's it going?'

He widened his eyes at me and I smiled because it was an expression which reminded me so much of Margi.

'Good, thanks.' He frowned and blew on his red hands. 'D'you want to help with this?'

I said sure and took a sheaf of the posters. They were for his band's next gig, with pictures of B-movie robots operating reel-to-reel tape players in front of a red sky cut with search-lights. I put one in my bag for my bedroom wall, then stuck the rest around a phone box.

'The smackheads'll love you for that,' he said.

'So what are you lot up to now?' I said. 'It's been a while since you played, hasn't it.'

'Yeah . . .' He squinted and considered this, pushing a wet kiss curl back out of his eyes, 'people ask me that . . . they say what direction are you going in and I say *many different directions*.' He looked down at his moccasins then up at the evening sky. 'Many different directions. North, south, east and west.'

I left Gene to his postering and walked on. I put my hands in my pockets and my head down and walked into the wind which never slackened. I schlepped down the steps at work. Kevin was sitting at the bar talking to Irene, who was busy making up her staff drink.

'Hey there,' said Kevin and he pointed at my All Stars.

'The shoes,' he said, 'the shoes have the moves.'

I smiled and did a little heel-toe jig while he kept pointing at my shoes. Soon enough Margi and Irene came out from behind the bar and pointed at my shoes as well.

One of our regulars, Vince, says that if you're feeling low you should 'put on a pair of tight shoes and go for a walk'. Vince is full of it sometimes. Another thing he harps on about is this story he's going to write one day, 'The Steepest Street in Manchester', about some road around the back of Victoria Station.

'It might be a story or a novel or maybe just a paragraph, but I quite like the title 'The Steepest Street in Manchester'. I tell you what, if you're ever feeling low you should get in a car at the top of that hill, take your foot off the pedal and go down with all the windows open, and when you reach the bottom, you'll be smiling!'

It sounds like a terrible title and a bad idea to me.

The shift went fast that night. I didn't get drunk and I didn't get tired, it was just the right side of busy. Margi and I went up the road to a club after work. We often go there on a Wednesday night with our wages, although it's a nasty joint. Margi bought us a cheap alcopop each and we both grimaced as, in a long established routine, we downed them in a single draught. We didn't like to walk around with those bottles.

I'm told I have a very serious look on my face when I'm dancing. When I was younger I never could dance, I was too self-conscious, too fraught. Now it's one of the joys of my life, especially dancing with Margi. I remember at the end of our first ever shift together she was drunk, and she took out the small smoke machine which is kept behind the bar, but rarely used, took it to the far corner of the room and plugged it in. It chuffed out a small white cloud of dry ice and she danced in it all on her own, swishing about her ragged trouser bottoms in an abbreviated twist. Bob the doorman was standing with one foot on the rail, supping his staff pint. He leant over and said to me, 'I don't want my troubles, I want hers. She dances hers away.'

I could only nod in agreement. When I've said that I was 'in thrall' of Margi part of what I mean is that I wanted to dance with her in that cloud of smoke, to be in her world.

So Margi and I danced. We've got some good moves between us, including the pointing at the shoes move (my invention) and the genuflecting move (her idea). Mostly though we just flicker our fingers in front of our eyes and look serious (so I'm told). Margi broke off from all this and raised her eyebrows at me meaningfully. Then she disappeared off towards the ladies. I looked where she'd been looking. Tony. A surprise. I took a deep breath.

I'd seen him only once since we split. He came into the bar one night and I just ignored him. Or maybe he ignored me. It's hard to tell. Either way we didn't speak. I let Margi serve him, and he went and sat down in one of the booths with his brandy and Coke, stretched his stupid skinny denim legs out under the table, and kept his thin blue anorak zipped right to the top. If we'd talked and I'd caught his eye I was afraid he would see that I was kicking at this wall of ice that has slammed between us for whatever reason I don't know. I'd have had to get drunk just to look at his face. Sometimes I wish I'd never seen his face.

Now he walked over.

'You were really cutting up that dance floor there, Carmel,' he said, pulling on his cigarette.

'All in a day's work,' I said, without looking

at him. Then I did look at him. I looked him up and down. I said, 'You're too cool for an establishment like this, surely.'

He grinned. 'I was going to say the same thing to you. So why are we here then?'

A good question. I considered it. 'To remind ourselves why not to come next week.'

'A-ha . . .'

He nodded over at a noisy huddle of lads who had sneaked take-aways in under their jackets.

'I wish I was a student,' he said, 'then I could afford pizza . . . and hair gel.'

I laughed and he leant in close. I could feel his breath on my neck as he spoke. 'I've got a book in my back pocket though . . .'

I shook my head. 'It means nothing, Tony. It means nothing. What book anyhow?'

'Oh, it's something you lent me.'

Just then I saw his friend coming over from the bar. I backed off quickly and gave a neat military salute.

'I'll check you later, Tony,' I said.

I turned away, flushed, and found Margi buying us some more drinks.

*

I woke up to the crashing sound of Irene dropping empty bottles into the skip. I opened one eye, and ran my tongue over my teeth and over the ulcers stinging on the roof of my mouth. I was curled up along the bench in one of the booths, Margi was opposite me. Fast asleep with her tongue hanging out she looked like a little dead dog. I sat up and was satisfied to find that I didn't have a hangover. But I rarely do these days. Irene came over and dropped something on the table in front of me. Looked like beads.

'Do these belong to either of you two dirty stop-outs?'

I picked the little things up, and held them in my palm. It took a moment to recognise them as three broken teeth. I took one and ran my finger along the sharp splintered edge. I winced.

'Found them in the gutter outside. Must have been a fight,' Irene said, shifting Margi's feet so she could sit at the table. 'I'm going to put them in the voodoo tin.'

This was a tall red tin, which once held an expensive bottle of whisky, and now stood on the top shelf behind the bar, full of all sorts of ephemera, odd things we'd found or been given. In a whimsical moment Margi, Irene and I put an eyelash each in there, too. My finest contribution is a small green notebook, which was wedged down the back of a seat when I cleared up one night. It's blank except for the first page

68

which is scrawled on in black ballpoint. It took me a while to decipher it. It says:

> *Important. Sat., approx. 8pm. U.F.O.s, about 2 or 3 flying around between, say, Arndale and Chinatown as far as London Rd., absolutely silent, like big dinner plates. Due to the colouring being akin to sky background it is at first hard to distinguish. Has anyone notified the police?! or the papers!? If possible meet me at The King, Oldham Street, soon.*

Complete gibberish, but I like it.

'Good night?' Irene said.

'Yeah. Except Tony was out with that simpleton waitress.'

'Who?'

'That stage-school twit.'

Irene frowned then nodded, '. . . always wears the hats.'

'Yeah. We should go up to her restaurant some time and lower the tone and show that flibber-tigibbet a thing or two.' I leant back and yawned. I knew I was going over the top but I couldn't help myself. I locked my hands behind my head.

'Dumped for a tap dancer. Despair reigns,' I said. Then, 'That sounds like a crossword clue.

Without an answer. There is no answer. It is beyond sense.'

'Were you okay?' Irene looked worried.

'Yes, I was okay. You think I did something rash. No. In fact I comported myself with enormous dignity.'

Irene smiled and nodded, 'Good.'

At this point Margi groaned and sat up stiffly. She pulled on the ends of her tatty hair. Her eyes were still closed.

'Good night?' Irene said.

'The police became involved,' she said. It was one of our routines. 'They searched us . . .'

I completed the sentence, '. . . and all they found was books and bottles . . .'

'. . . black eyes and broken dreams.'

Margi giggled and lay back down. I reached over the table and stroked her hair.

'You know, Carmel,' Irene said, 'Tony was kind of a simpleton himself. I always thought so . . .'

I sighed. 'I know you did. But I don't think that's it, Irene. I mean the first conversation we had was about goddamn Akira Kurosawa. And that's not it either. He had true wisdom. He just gives out an impression. When I first met you I thought you were about sixteen. I was impressed that you were reading a broadsheet. How old are you now anyway?'

'Twenty-five,' she said, and took the teeth and stood up.

★

It may have been that Thursday night, or it might have been the following week, or even the week after that (they're all shuffled up together), that Margi didn't show up for work. Her and Gene don't have a phone in their flat, so Irene stayed on to work the evening shift with me, and I said maybe Margi was just too hung-over to show, although it had never happened before. Irene and I didn't talk about it too much. I'd not worked with Irene very often but I always liked her. She's five foot nothing, red hair. She dresses like a skater: big jeans and lots of Stussy and shell-toe shoes. Also, she can play the piano. This is the only remnant of her genteel childhood in Cornwall as far as I can make out. She often sticks around drinking after her shift and she can sometimes be persuaded to sit at the jalopy of an instrument we have in the bar. It's wildly out of tune but all the better for it, I think. Sometimes she leans over her shoulder to announce the numbers, leering like the organist in Blackpool Tower Ballroom; sometimes if she's drunk she kicks the stool away like Jerry Lee Lewis and plays comedy boogie-woogie. Margi has this routine where she shakes her head and says, 'You've got the boogie, but you're losing your woogie,' and then Irene stops dead and scowls. She didn't play that night though; we just put a tape on and read and got drunk for free. Every time I heard the door open and looked up I expected to see Margi.

At half two I called a taxi. It arrived at half three by which time Irene and I were deeply drunk. I sat in the front. I half-recognised the driver and when I told him my address he said, 'Oh yes, I've taken you many times before, we always have a chat.'

I nodded and smiled. I was drunk and tired. His car smelt of polish, like it was fresh from the valet's. I guess he normally did the airport run. His plush leather seat was reclined so much as to be almost horizontal. He steered with one outstretched hand.

'You're pretty relaxed there,' Irene said from the back.

He purred, 'Yeah ... I love working the nights.'

'You still with your girlfriend?' I asked. It was a standard conversation opener with the taxi drivers.

'Yeah, I am,' he nodded, 'but we're rowing at the moment 'cause she doesn't want to come on holiday.'

'Why not?' Irene asked, leaning forward between the gap in the seats.

'My girlfriend's fifty,' he said. He spoke slowly. 'She's a great lady. I'm forty-four, she's fifty, and for eighteen years she was with this bloke, married, and in eighteen years he did nothing nice for her, he wasn't horrible, he didn't hit her, don't get me wrong, he just wasn't *nice* . . . and she doesn't know how to take nice now, that's how I see it. Doesn't know how to react. I've been seeing her five months and she's had a ring: £200, a bracelet: £200, three bunches of flowers, two boxes of chocolates, meals out, and other odds and sods on top of that,' he yawned and shrugged, 'but she doesn't know how to take it, she's not used to how I am yet. So . . . she doesn't want to come on holiday . . . because I'd be paying.'

Irene and I nodded in all the right places. Poor sod, I thought. Then I asked him if he'd had any trouble recently. Another standard question.

'Course I have,' he nodded slowly. 'Just last night some clown tried to do a runner on me. You can't carry weapons. That's a problem. But you can get around it. Just reach under your seat there, sweetheart.'

I leant forward and pushed my hand under

the seat. I pulled out a torch; heavy, with a long, thick handle; a cosh, to all intents and purposes.

I sucked air in through my teeth. 'You could do some damage with that I bet.'

I passed it back to Irene and we both cooed over it. Irene got the giggles first and then I did too, so I just faced forward and kept my eyes on the road, pretending to be absorbed by the sights of Upper Brook Street. There was hardly anybody about now. Under the dead neon sign of a club a girl was lying face down on the pavement, sprawled like a starfish. Another girl sat on the kerb next to her, bored, blowing smoke from her cigarette and making a call on her mobile. No answer.

The taxi slowed at some traffic lights and Irene leant forward and poked me in the ribs. 'Look at the state,' she said. 'It's that muso you pick-pocketed that time. The showboat.'

I looked where she pointed. It was him. She said, 'He tried it on with me as well that night, after you left. Waited 'til everyone had gone, 'til there was just me and him. I thought he seemed harmless enough. Next thing you know he's dropped his trousers. I just reached down and cupped his balls and said *Caesar, you are only a man . . .*'

I wasn't really paying attention to Irene, I was

74

watching that guy, although it was a bland enough sight. He was stumbling drunk along Oxford Road alone, holding onto the wall with both hands as he went.

5

I know only a handful of carefully dispatched details about Margi's past; baroque anecdotes which changed with each telling.

She grew up in Bolton, living with her dad, a derelict drunk, and her brother Elliott, who is twelve years older than her. I've never met him, but Margi's described him. She loves him to bits. He's six feet tall, blond, he's got a stutter and he blinks while he's trying to get his words out. Years ago he used to work on some government sponsored regeneration scheme, clearing waste ground near where they lived. He got made a charge hand because he'd never been in prison. If it rained, that was 'inclement weather' which meant everyone could sit in the hut and play poker for matchsticks, and that's where Margi used to go and pass the time when she skipped school. But it's always inclement weather in Bolton. So soon enough they all got the sack.

When she was fourteen Margi and her best friend Teresa formed a band. Well, nominally they formed a band. They got Elliott to take pictures of them together against derelict urban backdrops. Margi couldn't play an instrument – although a boy at her school once offered to buy her a glockenspiel if she slept with him. I was curious what had become of this Teresa, Margi's first confidante, but for a long time Margi wouldn't say, until one night she told me that reports had reached her of Teresa in Stoke University Students' Union, dancing with a guy who was wearing a rugby top. I didn't know what to say to that. I made her a drink.

Margi first started having nights out in Manchester when she was fifteen. At the Hacienda they called her 'the garage flower' and would let her in for free. Not unpredictably, she fast acquired a much older boyfriend. Mark Dalton. He was thirty-six. He liked people to see them out together at clubs so everyone could wonder what a pretty young thing like her was doing with him. And Margi liked the idea of this too. She liked him to look old, crumpled and unshaven. They went out together and had drunken, jealous rows. They caused scenes. She started staying at his place in Chorlton most nights, and she says *every morning* they'd take their caff breakfast, beans on toast in a polystyrene tray and cups of thick tea, into Southern Cemetery, sitting together on the wet grass and talking lofty nonsense. I'm sure it wasn't every morning, but what the hell. And it was this Mark, so she says, taught her the importance of always making a good entrance and a better exit. 'The entrance is important,' he'd say, 'but the exit is crucial.' When he finished with her, unceremoniously, she returned to his flat and left an orchid on his doormat, with a note instructing him to think of her while he watched it wither and die. 'Well, I was seventeen, I was a romantic . . .' she shrugs.

Was this a good exit from Margi? Maybe it was. Where was she? My heart thrummed in my stomach all afternoon. I felt uneasy and a little ashamed that I was thinking about it so much. I knocked on the door of her flat that evening on my way into work but there was no reply.

*

A couple of days later, at Irene's behest, we went looking for Gene's brother Arthur at Longsight Market, where I knew he ran a book and record stall. A bare-bulb sun hung beneath a slanting bank of black clouds; the rain made a static crackle as it hit the dirty pavement. The cold air carried out the stink of the meat counters and the grubby tarpaulin canopies above the fruit stalls held their own puddles. Irene and I sloped through the aisles. From nowhere a landslide of strawberries chased across our path. An old woman with a green beanie hat on leant over her trestle table to watch them get stood on. She sucked her teeth and shook her head and said to her husband, 'We'll never get to Madeira at this rate.'

Irene had called the owner, Mr Henrik, first thing to look after the bar for her until we could find Margi. Mr Henrik is a taciturn old man, he's hardly ever around. I like him though. He showed up growling, looked through the post and said, 'More bills, more bills, Merry Christmas.'

He wore a black overcoat and his longish grey hair was slicked back, still wet from the shower. He smelt like sandalwood. Irene had to show him how to work the coffee machine. He made me a cappuccino and it tasted pretty bad, gritty and weak, but I smacked my lips and gave him two thumbs up.

'Tip?' he growled. 'Tip?'

I patted my pockets and after a minute I offered him two pennies and a plectrum in a matchbox. My lucky pennies, a present from a long time ago.

'You can have my lucky pennies,' I said.

He frowned, 'Oh yeah, look where they've got you . . .'

I raised my eyebrows and smiled. 'Easy there, Mr Henrik.'

We found Arthur O'Brien after fifteen minutes' searching. I'd never met him before but felt sure I could recognise an O'Brien: big eyes, faraway look, an urban innocent. When I'd told Irene about Gene's brother Arthur she was disturbed.

'He's got a biological relative, that's wrong. I thought he'd been grown in a pod.'

I spotted him from a distance, using a black marker to draw sparks and lightning on a soggy cardboard box full of LPs. We went and leant on his counter. I looked through a stack of books while Irene talked to him.

'Hey there, Arthur?' she said, and he looked up and widened his eyes. 'I'm Irene, Margi's friend from work. We wondered where she'd got to. Did you see her and Gene this week?'

Arthur frowned and screwed his mouth up. Then he widened his eyes and smiled and said, 'Gene? Yeah. They went to Buxton for a holiday. Snowing there apparently.'

'Oh, right,' Irene said and nodded. 'Are they coming back?'

'We're playing in two weeks, so I guess they'll be there.'

Of course. I remembered the poster on my wall.

I bought a couple of books from Arthur and then we walked back up to the bus stop.

'Good for Margi,' I said. 'We can get Mr Henrik to help out 'til we find someone new, can't we?'

Irene shrugged. 'Well, we've no choice, have we.'

★

As far as friendships and relationships go, I've never gone in for visits and constant phone calls. The daily emotional weather report makes everything bland and cheap. Your feelings can seem so fragile and unlikely, why not keep them strange and beautiful instead of sharing them with anyone who'll listen. I think people should learn to spend more time in their own heads, they should come to their own terms. There are exceptions to that though.

I only ever visited Margi and Gene once. I went round on a Sunday evening to get some pills. Their living room walls are painted a vivid green and the skirting boards and ceiling are red. That night a couple of skinny candles stood on a low table in pools of amber light. Gene was sitting cross-legged on the floor, on the standard rented accommodation scratchy grey cord carpet, wearing his NASA jumpsuit and an ungainly pair of headphones. He was picking an aimless tune on his guitar, nodding to his music and staring out through the bars on their uncurtained bay window. The sky was a darkening mauve.

He looked up and blinked and smiled at me and took his headphones off but kept playing his guitar.

I sat down on the edge of the settee and warmed my hands on their gas fire. Margi went into the kitchen and got my pills from the tea caddy.

'Quiet night in?' she said as she picked a couple out of a small plastic bag and handed them to me.

'Yeah,' I nodded. 'Am I missing the point, do you think?'

She shrugged then went back into the kitchen and passed me out a mug of whisky. The mug was from the Granada Studios Tour and had a line drawing of Holmes and Watson reclining on stiff-backed armchairs and a short paragraph bordered with a William Morris vine: *Mr Sherlock Holmes and Dr Watson resided at 221b Baker Street from 1881 to 1904. The rooms they rented have been faithfully maintained to preserve their atmosphere and are open to the public.*

Margi sat on the arm of the settee, and we

chewed the fat for a while, about the movies I'd seen that day. Absently she reached over to Gene's guitar and twisted the keys one by one to slacken or to tighten his strings. He kept playing, untuned, and stared up at her, screwing his mouth up and making big eyes. She didn't look at him; she winked at me.

I could picture Margi and Gene in Buxton, wearing their matching hunter's hats; making angels in the snow, fallen back together against some low, soft slope.

★

Irene trained in graphic design, and she still does flyers and posters and the occasional record sleeve. But her most lucrative enterprise is a bus pass scam. She prints off Megariders and sells them for a pound a go from under the bar. We used some of hers on the bus back into town from Longsight. We sat on the back seat and I took out the two books I'd bought off Arthur: dog-eared, card-bound Graham Greenes, the flyleafs marbled with mould. I started reading one while Irene looked out of the window. People's clothes were drying, and the air filled with a cold humidity, the smell of fabric conditioner and mildew. I pointed out a passage to Irene: *It was as if this part of the world had never*

83

been dried in the flame when the world spun off into space: it had absorbed only the mist and cloud of those awful regions.

She nodded and looked around the bus and nodded again.

'What's it about,' she said, tapping the book.

'It's about . . . being an exile, I suppose.'

'Oh . . . I know about that,' she said.

'Why's that?'

She pulled at her stubby ponytail. 'Because, I can't go home anymore . . .'

'To Cornwall . . .'

'Mmm . . .'

I almost said 'Tony's from Cornwall, you know', but I thought better of it. 'Why not?' I said.

'Because . . . of the way I left. It's complicated. I went off the rails,' she said.

'And now . . .'

She rolled her eyes, 'Now . . . I'm just still lying on the embankment, I suppose.'

I laughed.

She went on, 'I've chilled out a lot since then, though. I'd only take drugs on special occasions now. Or if I was on the beach. I'll do anything if I'm at the beach, that's my trouble, I think, in essence.' She bit her lip as she considered this. 'Last time I was at home, all I ate from the

Tuesday night to the Saturday night was a peach.'

'A peach? . . . I thought you were going to say a piece of toast. A peach? A peach on the beach?'

'I was just flying around. I was scared. I thought I'd capsized my mind. Now I can't go back . . . and *I am that place*,' she said simply. She wiped a porthole in the steamed up window with the cuff of her dark blue anorak.

I glanced out and said, 'Increasingly, I think I am this place.'

She sighed and frowned and sunk down in her seat, putting her little trainered feet up on the seat in front. 'I hate it here sometimes. It's a fucking shithole.'

'Well, fiddle–di–dee,' I said, and mimed tying on a bonnet. 'Fine sentiments, Irene. But here we are getting the bus into town.'

★

Tony's band rehearse in a large, cold room above a run of garage lock–ups in Ardwick. You have to pick your way across the floor carefully because there are boards missing. I didn't want to hang out in there, although Tony always asked me.

I went up there once, after I'd been to a gig in town. I installed myself on the tatty brown sofa; the worn–shiny velour puckered with cigarette burns, sitting with my legs crossed and swigging the bottle of Tia Maria I'd been pulling on all day.

I hadn't asked Tony to come to the gig with me. I went on my own and stood in the dark to one side, near the front, with my hands in my pockets, stamping the rhythms with one heel. The American singer wore a dust-logged black baseball cap, his dark blond hair pressed flat in ragged pieces down his neck, in front of his ears. The peak was folded in the middle and shaded his eyes when he looked down, which he did most of the time. Towards the end of the set he played the song I'd come to hear. His fingernails brushed the wood of his guitar, tapping like morning rain on the window, then this song started to slap and clatter along. It felt nasty and unstoppable and I couldn't look away. The key crept up, he lifted his head then and his eyes were wounded spite; he sang, a hissing whisper, '*How-come-you're-not-ashamed-of-what-you-are?*'

How come you're not ashamed of what you are. Of what I am, *what I am*. I watch people that's what I am. I watched Tony. He was amiably drunk and he was arguing with his band, his shadow lurching across the wall behind him.

'Why do we have to play *this tune* or *that tune*,' he said. '. . . why can't we just play . . . music?'

I swigged at my bottle and as I swirled the sticky liquid round my teeth I thought, *Tony, you're going to wind up with some lovely long-haired free spirit, living in your house by the sea, a West Coast girl, nothing like me whatsoever, and I'm going to stick around here becoming some kind of a holy fool . . . I can see it all, I can see it all ahead.*

I felt serene to be thinking those thoughts. I felt a strange elation. When everyone else had left Tony came and sat next to me and put his arm around me and said, 'I'm really glad you're with me, Carmel.'

I felt like crying that he should say that to me but I smiled, and shrugged, and nodded, and held his free hand and stared straight ahead. I saw my own shadow against the stripes of light the blinds were throwing against the wall. To think. I fooled him.

★

I was remembering this on the bus and on a whim I stood up and said to Irene, 'Let's get off early. I want to show you something.'

'Do we have to? I want to go and get a drink.'

I gave her a look for that, she was being a real *mater dolorosa*, and that was my job.

We got out in Ardwick. The rebuilding hasn't reached out there yet, although in the middle distance you can see the cranes in town slowly seesawing above the low-rise skyline; the council blocks with their balcony and fire-escape exoskeletons painted royal blue. Irene followed me across a rain-slicked car park and a patch of litter-strewn scrub behind that. The Apollo points prow-like across this small municipal garden. The flowers in there make me think of the old recipe cards in the back of a kitchen drawer at my mum's; ragged carnations the colour of evaporated milk and tongue. There were dozens of cans in the bracken, held up by the dead black branches. I walked fast and kicked one ahead of me. Suddenly Irene stopped with her hands in her pockets and stray hair blowing into her face. She shook her head.

'Oh, I know where we're going. Bad idea. Bad idea.'

It was a bad idea, but that wasn't the point.

'Just to listen, Irene, come on. Come on.' I stretched out my arms to her. 'He's my Cornwall.'

Irene twisted her heels about then sighed and strode to catch up.

'Okay, Carmel.'

We sat together outside the rehearsal room in the cold.

'Listen to that voice,' I said. 'You don't learn that, you're given that.'

I felt stricken, I hugged my knees.

'Yeah, yeah,' Irene said.

She was busy key-scratching our names on the red lock-up door.

6

Mr Henrik has owned this place with his older brother since the sixties, when it was a more up-market establishment. Somewhere behind the bar, in the cardboard folder with the bills and the fire regulations, there's an ancient, worn-soft clipping from the *Evening News*; a grainy photograph of George Best sitting in one of the booths, complete with a Page Three lovely and a champagne-glass pyramid.

Margi once told me that Mr Henrik's brother disappeared in 1983, to his complete indifference, and has not been heard of since, except for a cryptic letter from some nuns in Fairbanks, Alaska, five years later, who claimed to have found him and taken him in, and wrote to reassure Mr Henrik that he was in good health and in good hands.

Mr Henrik will only ever hire girls for behind this bar, and it's always by word of mouth rather than a card in the Job Centre. Irene and I discussed this at work the night we'd been out to Longsight. We turned over a few names.

'We've done a good job of ruining our own lives,' I said. 'We should branch out and ruin someone else's.'

'You've got quite a downbeat disposition, haven't you,' she said.

I was aware that we were amplifying each other's bad mood. I told Irene I was going to go and sit outside for five minutes. I poured out a Baileys and brandy and took it upstairs with me. I said hey to Bob on the door and then went and sat on the kerb. I thought about all the sorry soldiers who wash up in my bar night after night, lip-synching the same tired apocrypha, the sententious excuses, the green-eyed lies, wanting me to know when and how and why. What did they really think? And what was it like for them to look at each other and see themselves? That must be the worst thing. I felt a frightening sob lurch in my stomach, but I dug my fingernails into my palms and stopped it dry. I've got no right to get upset about anything. I took a deep breath, then I lolled my head back and tipped my drink into my mouth and held it there for a moment, warm and sweet, before swallowing, staring up at the clear sky. I stood up suddenly and made as if I was going to throw my glass into the gutter, but I just tossed it up behind my back and caught it with my other hand, cocktail waitress style.

When I went back inside, Vince was talking to Irene, and she was trying to give him half an ear while serving other customers. He was irritating her, I could tell. His soft, short hair was sticking up in sweaty wisps, he was smiling beatifically, and waving his empty beaker about as he talked.

'When we had music lessons in school, I didn't pay attention, I used to sit at the back of the class and play paper and comb . . .'

I went to the side of the bar and started tearing up the boxes the beer bottles had come in, then flattening them out so they could be pushed into the skip. The cardboard's thick, so when I'm doing it I set my face mean because it makes it easier.

Vince called over, 'All right Frosty-Arse?'

He called me this to try and get a rise out of me; he hated it when we weren't paying him attention.

Irene started talking to a couple of her friends at the other end of the bar and I saw Vince hop off his stool and hove towards me.

'All right Frosty?' he said.

'Not so bad,' I said. 'You?'

'Good, thanks.'

I kept tearing the boxes.

'Having fun?' he said.

'Damn straight,' I smiled at him, 'It's very cathartic.'

'What is? Menial work?'

He laughed then skipped off back to the bar. It's always the way. The sentimental ones are the ones who turn nasty.

There was a full complement of familiar faces lined up along the ledge that night. I got bought a few drinks and I felt okay. I put one of my tapes on: loud fast music, 'drums, bass, guitars and shouting', Margi used to call it, with two thumbs up. I smiled at everyone I served.

★

Tony was a great drunk. Good-natured and garrulous, as it should be. One of our first times out together, we spent the afternoon at an expensive bar down on Deansgate Locks, because I'd said we should go and look at the glamour. We were sitting out in the sun, people-watching and eavesdropping and shooting the breeze, and I was so nervous, and I couldn't stop smiling. Tony got into a conversation with the people on the table next to us. Not about anything, just banter. I remember him saying to them: 'I'm well aware that there are people in this country reading

Chaucer, checking out the *Financial Times* and worrying about the Presidential election in America. But the large majority aren't: they're eating fish and chips and digging up roads . . .'

He was tipping his bottle right back between his teeth, and grinning at everyone, and I was laughing. He reached over the table and held my hand. When he was drunk, he said things like, 'I'm not very educated, Carmel. I can lift heavy things though.' And, 'I find life quite confusing, you know, Carmel.'

Then I'd narrow my eyes at him and say, Well, I'll light a candle for you, dear heart.

★

I told Irene I was going to ask my friend Shelley Kane if she wanted a job. Well, I say friend. I knew Shelley as a sulky usherette up at the Odeon. I'd often seen her when I was walking up to work. She'd be standing outside the cinema on her break, her arms folded, smoking and tapping her foot. I always pointed at the posters and asked her what was good, but she'd only ever have seen the last fifteen minutes or the first fifteen minutes, and she'd generally say they were complete shit. 'Fair enough,' I'd say.

When I go to the pictures I always sit in the very middle of the front row. On the rare occasions

94

when Margi came with me she would too; Katja would feel self-conscious and want us to stay at the back. Tony and I never went to the pictures together. One time, as I sat down alone in a nearly empty afternoon show I heard some kid at the back say 'Daft cow.'

So I twisted around in my seat and flicked him and his girlfriend the Vs.

I was only in there killing time. The film was so terrible I was throwing popcorn at the screen. I felt bad afterwards and went to pick it up again. That's how I met Shelley. She also works a few days a week at a chain coffee shop down by King Street. And she hates it there, too. When I saw her next I said, 'How's the mochaccino racket?'

And she near enough snarled, 'Supervisor came in the other day,' she shook her head, 'in disguise . . . he timed me and said it took me seventeen seconds to smile, this is unacceptable etcetera . . .'

The girl with the seventeen-second smile. I should tell Vince about that some time, it might make a nice companion piece to his 'Steepest Street . . .' opus.

I asked her about working in our bar and she took a moment, chewing on one of her thumbnails. Then she shrugged, and whistled, and said sure.

★

I was working on my own the next night, but it was quiet so that didn't matter. Kevin showed up late, carrying a brown leather portfolio brief-case and when I asked what he'd like he said, 'I'd like a wide woman in a narrow bed, Carmel!' and I rolled my eyes.

We played draughts over the bar. I couldn't find the counters so we used beer caps. Gold foil for him and red for me. I'm a member of the draughts team up at The Castle on Oldham Street. I only joined on a whim but I go most Sundays and sit in silent contemplation in the back room with all the old-timers. They like me in there. They've even asked me to go and play in a tournament at Longsight Library.

'Where's Margi these days?' Kevin said.

'She's gone,' I said. 'But there's a new girl starting tomorrow night. Shelley Kane. She works up at the cinema at the moment. She's a sulky usherette.'

I could read his thoughts then. He was picturing a young Voluptua with a tray of ciga-rettes and a pill-box hat, swirling a dancing tinkerbell spot of torchlight through dust motes and whispers of blue smoke.

I pointed at Kevin's briefcase and said, 'What's that all about, Kevin?'

Without saying anything he reached down and unzipped it and then passed me an impressive charcoal and pastel picture of himself, in his raincoat and his red Hawaiian shirt, with a pink smudged nose and a rueful expression.

'I'm taking evening classes up at Stockport College,' he said with a smile.

I squinted to read out the title which he'd pencilled in one corner next to his loopy signature. '"Self-Portrait After a Few Beers?"' I said.

He nodded seriously. I changed my mind about Kevin. The man is a poet.

7

Shelley Kane started work on Bonfire Night. At the end of the shift we went outside and put rockets in bottles and fired them off. It was my idea but Shelley lit them, because I was too nervous. To be safe, she tucked all her long, wavy brown hair into her hat. It was a fine hat, a peaked army-green wool affair. She looked mean in her drainpipe jeans and pointy shoes. I sat on the kerb and made explosion noises when the fireworks went off, and then flickered my fingers as the gold and silver rained down.

When Shelley had turned up Irene was already drunk after an eight-hour shift with just three customers. She phoned me and told me to come in early because she was going stir crazy.

Before she left she poured out half a shot of Archers, dipped in her fingers and dabbed some on her neck and wrists.

'I've got a date,' she said.

I smiled but I wasn't in the mood for it. I felt . . . a ferocious boredom.

Then all night long Vince was saying to Shelley, '*She* thinks I'm a misogynist. What's a misogynist?' And whenever either of us had a break he said, 'Look at you! Leisure City!' And when he left, at last, at midnight he said, 'I'm off now. Back to Work City.' He's an infant. A moon-sick baby that wants to cry itself hoarse. When Gareth has cunts in his restaurant he says he's extra nice and it undermines them. He thinks that's the noble way to be. I'm afraid I have different impulses. Occasionally I lose my rag and I hate it when I do. I've screamed at people, I've thrown drinks in their faces. Bad behaviour, you'd better believe it. But more often I let them say what they like and then, later on, I get like a geisha on my hands and knees picking up broken glass and torn cigarette ends, sweeping up smashed bottles into a dustpan, mopping up spills and sick, and making them see me do it and look how young and pretty I am on my hands and knees in their shit.

So, I was happy to be out of there, sitting in the ice cold, sober, watching the fireworks and not talking. Shelley's great that way. She just stood with her hands in her back pockets, looking at the sky with no expression on her face.

★

I got up early the next day and went into town, planning to spend the day in the cafe at Victoria Station with my books: a Dashiell Hammett and a Turgenev.

I had on my jeans and All Stars and a crumpled up fitted grey shirt with my leather jacket. I'd plaited my hair and pinned it up on either side of my head. I don't mind saying I looked pretty good.

At the station I bought a large tea and a packet of three biscuits.

'Can you leave the bag in,' I said to the man at the till.

'Just like at home,' he said, 'so the spoon'll stand up.' And I nodded and smiled.

I went and sat near the window. I took my books out and put them on the table, but didn't open one straight off. I leant back in my plastic chair and looked up through the rain-streaked, domed glass ceiling, and then out across the way at the building site: another cinema. The window was a slab of grey, it wasn't letting in light. The dulling indoor atmosphere suited my mood, though. And my tea tasted like an elixir.

I sat in Victoria for a couple of hours reading. I saw two middle-aged men, both in tobacco-brown, double-breasted suits, meet up and swap rare stamps, pulling them from envelopes in plastic carrier bags. I saw the man from the till put down the huge bag of change he was shouldering to chase a pigeon away from under a table. He clapped his hands behind it, and it hopped and fluttered forlornly out onto the concourse.

I left at around three, and walked up towards town. I decided to bar hop until work, starting with the Cornerhouse cinema bar. I know the bloke who works there, Nelson, so we chewed the fat for a while and he slipped me some free drinks. Nelson's only eighteen, but he's very careworn. I sat behind him on a bus once, before I'd ever spoken to him. He was leaning forward on his umbrella, but from where I was sitting it looked like a walking stick and my heart went out to him.

Nelson took me out driving once. When he turned up and beeped outside my flat I was ready for a road trip: I had a map, a bag of apples, a bottle of vodka and my transistor radio to put on the dash. But I soon got bored, sitting folded into the front seat of his tiny car. We stopped at a pub up in the Pennines. They only had beef and onion flavour crisps. 'How perfect is that?' I said. After that, as if we didn't have enough momentum to get over the mountains, we just drove right back to Manchester.

While me and Nelson were talking I'd been watching the only other customer, a kid sitting on a bench at the back of the room, and I'd decided to give him the eye. He had a look about him: goofy curly brown hair, wearing red All Stars, jeans which were just too short for him and a brown blanket coat. I always pay attention to people who wear All Stars. He was reading the newspaper and drinking a coffee, holding his cup like a glass; that is, not using the handle. I liked that. With my elbows on the bar and one foot on the rail I looked over at him then looked away, then looked at him again then looked away. He looked up at me, then looked down again, smiling. I twitched my eyebrows at Nelson, he tutted at me and then went and stacked glasses up noisily. I turned to the window. The buses slowed for the junction as they passed the bar's glass front, swilling the puddles over the pavements. Faces stared out and I stared back. But the window was a mirror as well, and I saw All Stars rubbing his wrist against his forehead as he flicked the pages of his paper, not reading it.

Then he pushed his chair out to stand up and walked over to put his cup on the bar. He smiled at me. A pretty nice smile. He leant his elbows on the bar and looked at me properly.

'Hey there,' he said.

An American. You can call me crass because my heart leapt . . .

'Hey there,' I said, 'I'm Carmel.'

'Lucas,' he said and clicked his empty cup against mine, as outside another audience drew up and the gutter puddles bashed woozily over the kerb.

'Would you like to go and get a drink someplace else, Carmel.'

I winked at Nelson as we left. It occurred to me that Lucas might be putting the accent on for a lark. That he was really from Urmston. But as I followed him to the exit I thought, no, this kid even walks like a cowboy.

As we walked I asked Lucas what he was doing in England.

He said, 'Well, I'm on vacation, kind of. I flew in here, two weeks ago, I went to London, to Bristol, to Liverpool, and back here today because I fly home in the morning . . . Does this seem strange to you?'

'No,' I said, 'not at all. I think that's the kind of thing I'd do. Go on a trip on my own in November. Definitely. If I could ever save my money.'

He bit his lip. 'Really?'

I grinned and nodded.

Lucas was twenty years old, like me. He was from Austin, Texas, but, 'majoring in sculpture at NYU'. We had a good time out drinking and shooting the breeze. At a small bar behind the Bridgewater Hall he drank rum and Cokes and I had the same. He had a way of scratching the back of his neck and pressing his lips together when he was thinking. But as he talked he shrugged a lot and smiled a lot and waved his hands about. He really had a lot of energy. We talked about the usual: books, films, music. Yes, he liked all those things a lot, but, as he said, nodding vigorously, 'My main thing is really the sculpture. I love to sculpt!'

He asked me if I played an instrument and I said no, and he shook his daft curly hair and said, 'Well, you know that's a waste of two hands . . .'

I thought about it and said, 'Well, I play the typewriter . . . does that count?'

A lie. Although I was on a record once, incidentally. One of our old regulars was making an album and asked me to do some vocals for him. I said sure and arranged to meet him one afternoon outside the Woolworth's on Cheetham Hill Road. 'I'll be reading the *Guardian* and . . . holding a pork pie,' he said. We went into a studio behind some garages and I just had to say the word 'heartbreaker'. I said it soft and slow and matter of fact.

It's a nice track. We put it on in the bar sometimes.

Lucas said that playing the typewriter counted
all right. He was sitting cross-legged on his seat.
He closed one eye and said, 'You know, Carmel,
I think you need to consider this possibility: that
the people you run with just aren't sophisticated
enough for you. You should, you know, next
time they want you to stay out getting crazy
drunk, you should, you know, say Fuck you man,
I'm not gonna spend the last of my dough on
another shitty whisky . . . I want to buy avocados
Tuesday!'

He finished his drink, then picked up my glass
and stood up to go to the bar.

While he was gone I called Irene and said I
was ill. The first time I've ever done that. But
as I said to Lucas as we stumbled up to his
room in the Midland Hotel, hours later, with
two bottles of wine in a Spar carrier bag . . .
Well, you've got to make the most of life, haven't
you?

His hotel room was very warm. Lucas took
off his jacket and his jumper and put them over
the back of a chair. Then he took his shoes off
and threw them under the TV. I did the same
and went and pulled the nylon cord which
opened the sheeny chintz curtains. From the

window I could see the library and right up to Piccadilly. A new perspective on the city.

Lucas brought two squat glasses from the bathroom, sat on the edge of the bed and unscrewed the cheap wine we'd bought.

'Can I know your second name,' he said, as he poured it out.

'McKisco,' I said.

'McKisco. So you're what, Irish?'

'No. I don't know what I am.'

You can guess what I felt. When I put four fingers on his cheek, my thumb under his chin and one knee up on the tucked-in covers.

*

Lucas noticed my tattoo. It made him laugh. Getting a tattoo was Margi's idea but I didn't object. We were so drunk that we climbed up the stairs to the tattoo parlour, using our hands as well. Margi got a tiny, ink-blue butterfly, and in the same place I got the title of a Tom Waits song, in clumsy capitals along the base of my spine: INNOCENT WHEN YOU DREAM. I always ask Irene to play it on the piano in the bar. I probably should have got a picture but I got words. There were two men working; father and son. Margi was wearing her trousers so she only had to push them down a little way when she leant over the bench. I had my space cadet dress on and I had to push it right up. I kept catching Margi's eye and she raised her eyebrows at me and then couldn't stop giggling and the old guy kept telling us to keep still. I guess my tattoo could be seen as embarrassing. But it meant something to me at the time, so I'm not embarrassed.

I said to Lucas, 'Tell me a story from your life.'

He put his hands up behind his head and said, 'Well . . . I remember once when I was in kindergarten. It was recess, and I was staring over at this girl that I wanted to like me, and as I crossed the playground I walked into a pole, and, gosh,' here he closed his eyes, 'I've been awkward around girls ever since.' He reached up and touched his lip and looked over at me. 'Your perfume is . . . tasty,' he said. 'I have a tang in my mouth.'

A twenty-year-old Texan with a mouthful of my cheap scent. Life was good.

Turning over with his back to me he pulled my arm around over his stomach. Just like Tony used to do. That's what it made me think.

'Sleep well,' he said.

'Yeah,' I said, pulling in closer to him, and then, biting my lip so as not to laugh, I said a line I nicked from one of mine and Margi's routines. I said, 'dreaming of your ass'.

'Why?' he sighed. 'Because its curves are sweet? Like a Cadillac? Like a Chevrolet?'

*

I woke up early. I couldn't hear any traffic, just the sound of my eyelashes scratching against the pillowcase, which smelt so clean. I saw Lucas's curly head in front of me, I'd forgotten what he looked like, I realised. I looked at the back of his head, at his rich, curly hair, wondering if he was awake as well. I sat up and grimaced at myself in the big mirror at the end of the bed, tidied my hair then lay back down and looked at the ceiling. I breathed in the quietude, the smell of the clean cotton sheets. I guess because he'd heard me shifting about, Lucas rolled over and pushed himself up on his elbows and smiled at me. His face looked crumpled and sleepy still.

'There's a strange girl in your bed,' I said, squinting one eye up, and he grinned some more.

*

He got up first and dressed, then cowboy-walked over to the window, pulling back the net to look out. The damp had held the creases in his jeans: crazy zigzags at the backs of his knees. He scratched his neck.

'I had some strange dreams last night, you know,' he said. 'Nightmares. I couldn't get back to sleep.'

'You should have woken me then,' I said. I tried to sound casual but I felt terrible all of a sudden. I sat up and pulled the sheet right up and round me.

He turned around and smiled. 'Well, no, you were sleeping pretty soundly.'

I shrugged. 'Do you want to go out and get coffee then?' I said.

He nodded.

We went into a small Italian café opposite Central Library.

He took his coffee black with one sugar. On his first sip he winced. 'I have, like, no taste buds left,' he said.

The blonde Australian girl behind the counter laughed at him and he stuck his tongue out then smiled.

We took our cardboard cups to a table outside, although it was really too cold for it.

'So,' he said, 'Carmel McKisco . . . where would you live if you could live anywhere?'

I thought about this for a while.

'For me obviously it's Disneyland,' he said. 'This is terrible coffee, don't you think?'

I took a breath. 'I'd like to go to New York

and get a bar job there . . . I'd like to retire to Cornwall . . . I'd like to live in the wilderness like in *Badlands*, like Jesus Christ.'

'Oh,' he shook his head, 'you know . . . I think you're a city girl . . . and what does Jesus Christ have to do with this?'

'He went to the wilderness. Get thee behind me Satan etcetera . . .'

'Yeah, I remember being told about that once . . . by a priest. But you can quote scripture . . .'

'No,' I shook my head, '*Jesus wept*, that's the only scripture I quote regularly.'

At this point a mangy little grey dog trotted across from the war memorial and jumped up to Lucas's chair. He scratched its flannely ears and then grimaced at me. He kept petting it while he was talking.

'I like dogs,' he said, 'but not when they climb me . . . maybe that's what New York did for me . . . pets are great though, they remind us what a fucked up species we are . . . I prefer cats to dogs they're . . .'

I sighed. 'What are you now, an observational comedian?'

'Yeah . . .' He smiled and shrugged. And then he told me a joke. And I can't remember it. You know, I'd give anything to be able to remember that joke.

By and by, when the coffee was long finished, and with the wind trying to blow the empty cups off the table, he asked me, 'So what are we going to do now? Am I just never going to see you again?'

I didn't answer. I shrugged.

He had to leave for the airport and I said I'd leave him to pack up. I was going to go visit my mum.

He made me show him where I was going on the Metrolink map. Then we sat down on the edge of the platform to wait. I hugged my knees and shivered.

'What are you feeling right now?' he said.

I wasn't sure what I was feeling.

'I'm sorry,' I said, 'I'm really not very articulate . . .'

He raised his eyebrows at me.

I patted my knees and took a breath and said, 'Okay. I tell you what. If I've got a pen in my bag I'll write down my number, but otherwise that'll be that.'

I pulled my bag onto my knees and opened it. He leant over my shoulder as I looked. I always have three or four pens in my bag, so this was not so grandiose a gesture as it may seem. Except, for once, for the first time, as I scrabbled, slowly, through the books and the make-up and the tampons, there weren't any pens. There wasn't a pen. I hoisted the bag back over my shoulder. I couldn't argue with that. I'd set myself up. I looked at Lucas and shrugged and he looked at me the same way I was looking at him.

My tram pulled in. We shook hands and then said goodbye and shook hands again, then Lucas hugged me, then I turned away first.

And when I got to Whitefield my mum wasn't even in. She'd gone out to buy paint, Frank said. They were redecorating.

'Will you tell her I called round,' I said.

'If I remember,' he said, and took his plate of toast up to his bedroom.

All the living room furniture was covered in white sheets. I sat down on the shrouded settee with a cup of tea. I unveiled the sideboard to get a Biro from the drawer, intending to put it in my bag later. There was a pile of newspapers on the table. I flicked through them while I drank my tea, found the crossword and chewed on the pen in between filling in clues. Suddenly I tasted something cold and sticky, metallic and fragrant. I put a finger up to my mouth and then looked at it. *That's done it*, I thought, and got up and went to look in the bathroom mirror. My tongue was blue and the gaps between my teeth were stained. I also had a blue mark in the middle of my lower lip. There was no question of washing it off. I kicked at the sink and then I looked at myself again and had this thought: *somebody really should kiss me now.*

Walking down the deserted residential streets back to the Metrolink I could hear tired arguments and radio chartshows drifting into the scrubby front gardens. I looked through swagged curtains into frumpy front rooms, into rooms that were dark save for the garish, ghostly flickering of the TV.

In the street light, a sudden shower of thin rain looked like ticker tape floating down. I tilted my head back, opened my mouth and stuck out my blue tongue, letting it drip in.

When I got back into town I went into Central Library, up to humanities on the third floor and looked up New York in a huge ring-bound atlas. I needed a whole table to open it out. Obviously I know where New York is, but I wanted to see it on the page, for some reason. I put a finger on Manchester and a finger on New York, and scored a flight path with my thumbnail.

When I got into work Irene said, 'What happened to you?'

I said, 'Oh, a real tragedy,' and shook my head. 'Romeo and Juliet in baseball boots. I'll tell you about it some other time.'

Mopping up the coffee grounds from under the machine at the end of the night I remembered the way the black hair on Lucas's stomach had swam and swirled and stuck.

★

The next night I was working with Shelley again. When she arrived she seemed even moodier than usual. She put her bag and coat and hat under the bar then ducked out again and asked Irene for a cup of tea.

'Leave the bag in, will you . . .' she said and then huffed as she pushed it about with her teaspoon.

'Sorry about the other night,' I said. 'Were you all right on your own?'

'Yeah,' she said, shaking her head. 'Let me just light up and I'll tell you what happened.'

She took a cigarette from the packet of Embassy in her shirt pocket and then started talking without lighting it, leaving it hanging from her bottom lip.

'I haven't been able to stop thinking about this,' she said and frowned. 'This woman came in, fifty-odd, on her own, and she was trying it on with every bloke in the place, sitting next to them and they'd ignore her. Mr Henrik was stood talking to Bob at the door and they were

114

taking the piss, laughing at her. She started dancing on her own and they started clapping. And I was kind of taking the piss too because I just thought: old lush with maroon hair. Sorry,' she said and shook her head and frowned. I could see her biting her lip and trying not to cry. 'But I can't stop thinking about it, I couldn't get to sleep all last night. All she wanted was a bit of fucking company. God it's awful. We were all being shitty to her and she realised, that's . . . that's the thing, suddenly she knew and she came up to the bar and said to me, Why are you doing this?'

Shelley pressed the heels of her hands into the hollows of her eyes. Irene went round to sit next to her.

'Hey, it's all right,' she said. 'She'll wake up today and she won't remember.'

Shelley was really crying, sniffing and shaking her head.

'All she wanted was to have a good time . . . She was telling me she'd lost her kid or something, I couldn't follow, but she just wanted to pick someone up and get shagged or whatever, and Bob and Mr Henrik . . . She was pathetic enough, it wasn't called for.'

She stood up and went to the Ladies. Irene exhaled.

'Bloody hell,' she said, and turned and took some money from the till. 'I'll go and get her something from Spar. What does she like?'

'Don't know,' I said, because I didn't. 'Cigarettes . . . erm . . . get a film magazine and some fruit or something.'

Irene nodded and then went up.

When Shelley came back she looked better. She peeped through her hand held in front of her face in mock shame.

'Sorry,' she said, and smiled. 'I came over all unnecessary. I must be sentimental or something.'

She laughed and ruffled her choppy fringe about.

'S'all right,' I said.

*

I went round to Shelley's flat in Collyhurst after work that night to watch some videos.

'I live with my brother, Stanley,' she told me in the taxi, 'which might sound awful but it's actually great. I used to be out on the town all the time when I was by myself. Pissed. I ended up in this house in Gatley for a while, with a load of people all doing glue, and they weren't kids either, and I just wondered, what the fuck am I doing? Now I go home and we have nice meals and talk about our day. I don't ever get drunk anymore. Just smoke. When I couldn't sleep last night I was just jumping about on my mattress smoking, for about three hours, just in my hoody and my knickers. Stan looked in and shook his head at me. It was funny.'

It did sound nice, I suppose.

'I don't really speak to my brother these days,' I said. 'We're very different.'

Frank unnerves me because he seems too big for that house now. When I called round I didn't like seeing his huge trainers by the front door, his big leather jacket hanging over the bottom banister. Made me think my dad was back. Frank and I can't ever get on because we saw those same things; what my dad did to Mum, and then her not quite managing after he died. Growing up together in that miserable place with the constant fear of him turning on us or Mum and feeling that nagging guilt about the bland fact of a failed family. Because it is bland. I'm sure similar things were happening in a lot of the houses on our old street and the new one too. Frank and I know things about each other. It's a minefield. I don't need that in my life.

Not so with Shelley and Stanley though. I sat on the sofa of their eighth-floor flat with Stan while Shelley got us all cups of tea. He looked a lot like her; a few years older, a little plumper. He was wearing jeans and a band T-shirt, green slippers and a pair of glasses on a gold chain round his neck. He tipped his ash into a saucer on the arm of the sofa, which was covered in a nasty psychedelic throw. I asked him where he worked and he told me he was doing some shifts at a chain bar in town.

'It's all right,' he said. 'Basically it's like Chorlton Street bus station, but the beer's in glasses not cans. It's Rockports, trackies, Ben Shermans, leather jackets, shaved heads, scars . . .'

'And that's just the women,' I said, before he did. He laughed.

Checking that Shelley wasn't listening he said, 'Get this, Carmel: when I was about nine Shelley said to me, *You've got a willy what have I got?* But I wouldn't say it. She kept pestering me, kept asking me, *You've got a willy what have I got?* and eventually, nearly crying, I said . . .' and here he pulled a pathetic face, '*vagina*, and she screams up the stairs, *Mum, Stanley said the F word.*'

I laughed. 'So,' I said, in a serious tone of voice, 'have you had screwed up feelings about your sister ever since?'

I mimed pointing a microphone at him. He leant in.

'Oh yeah.'

I pulled the mike back to me. 'And how did these feelings between you manifest themselves, Mr Kane?'

And back to him. He frowned. 'Sex. Mainly.'

Shelley came back through the screen door with three mismatched mugs on a tray. She narrowed her eyes and we grinned at her from the settee.

'What?' Stan said.

I stood up and took a cup with the bag still bobbing on the surface.

'Can I have a nosy round then?' I said.

Shelley sat down. 'Yeah, go for it,' she said. 'It's fairly underwhelming accommodation, but we do have a balcony.'

'Very glamorous,' I said.

I stooped down and scanned along her book-shelves and then flicked through her records. I found something quite interesting there, in fact.

On the windowsill there was a collection of 1940s plastic cocktail shakers and an ice bucket shaped like a pineapple. There were jumpers stuffed along the bottom of the plywood front door, to keep the stabbing draught out. Stanley got up and knelt by their overladen video shelf.

'What are you up for, Carmel,' he said. 'Intellectual stimulation or dumb fun?'

'Oh . . . dumb fun's all right,' I said, leaning on the cold radiator. 'I'll just put my brain in that pineapple.'

Shelley raised her eyebrows. 'No thanks. Put *Harold and Maude* on, Stan.'

A surprise.

'That's got to be one of my favourite films,' I said and Shelley nodded.

So we watched that and a couple more. Shelley and Stanley passed a joint between them and we all drank tea and talked and then went out and stood crowded on their tiny balcony to watch the muted sunrise through columns of blown rain.

It was a good night. But I couldn't help remembering those times last year when I'd go back to Margi's when the shift finished, with a bottle from work and cheap mixer from the Spar.

I can see her standing up on the settee to make a point, flicking her streaming hair over her shoulder and sticking her little finger out as she swigged the liquor from a tea-stained mug. And me crawling across the dusty carpet with a leery look on my face. Rolling over with a tingle in my fingers and a cigarette behind each ear. And I don't even smoke. We both got little bellies from drinking and we'd poke where they stuck out and decide to drink our vodka with prune juice. Once I said, 'Look at my derelict physique, Margi. I'm losing it. It's lost.'

And she said, 'Well at least you're not like me: a distended cranium and a withered heart.'

She was still smarting from that older guy in Chorlton back then.

That's when things are meaningful. With a friend in the witching hour and some music on that seems to have come from nowhere. From space. From the wilderness. I remember one song, all crashing cymbals and a whip–crack pace. It went:

> *If I don't start crying it's because that I have got*
> *   no eyes,*
> *My Bible's in the fireplace and my dog lies hyp-*
> *   no-tised,*
> *Through a crack of light I wasn't able to find my*
> *   way,*
> *Trapped inside a night but I'm a day,*
> *And I go 'oo-bip-bip-oo-bip-bip yeah!'*

Margi would switch the light off if she wanted me to really appreciate a song. Then she'd slowly turn up the volume on the record player so the headphones seemed very warm in my ears.

In the morning we would walk out in the unnatural light and up into town for the sake of it. We went in the Arndale Centre toilets to put our faces on. Silty-rain footprints crowded around the exits; dispersed along the strip-lit shop-lined corridors and up and down the escalators.

I walked back from Shelley's that next morning, swinging a small plastic bag carrying a record I'd borrowed from her. 'Factory Greyness' was a very early song by that Macclesfield band I was so hung up on. I'd read about it, read the lyrics, but never heard it, because it was never properly released. Shelley had got a copy through a friend of a friend. It was a song about visiting Ian Curtis's grave, something Steven used to do a lot according to all those old interviews, with their moody photos and punchy pull-out quotes. There was a line from that song that had always stuck in my mind, though: *Passing by your modest kerbstone*. I like that line a lot.

I know in the big picture my thing about that band, and my thing with Tony, possibly shouldn't mean so much. But, you see, the point is, I'm not in the big picture. I'm in Manchester, and I can't earn enough to leave just yet. For now these are my parameters: the spokes of the bus routes out to the A roads; those sparse stretches lined with derelict pubs and retail parks. Precisely the same to the north, south, east and west. For now I walk around through the scraping wind, through puddles full of brick dust, often with my feet so cold and sodden; the flesh of my toes like soaked cotton wadding spun around the bones.

It was with these ideas in mind that I called Shelley up, as soon as I got back to my flat, wringing out my ponytail as I spoke to her. I proposed something that I wasn't really sure if she'd be into. But she was and I was pleased about that. So: another excursion to Macclesfield.

8

I told Shelley about my eighteen-hour love affair with Lucas. I called him 'an itinerant bow-legged oil baron's son' and she raised her eyebrows. I asked her if she'd ever been to New York. She said, yeah, she went with Stanley two years ago. She shrugged her bony shoulders in her anorak and said, 'You know, Carmel, New York's just like Manchester, only it's taller.'

That was her final word on the subject. It was early on a Thursday evening and we were on the train, on our way out to Macclesfield to find our old hero, Steven Unsworth. It was weird that we should have this past in common, Shelley and I. Or maybe not so weird.

I'd bought half a dozen of the cheapest alcopops from the Thresher's at Piccadilly. Shelley uncapped them with the bottle opener on her key ring.

'I think you'll have to stay drunk so we don't sack this off as a bad idea,' she said.

'Maybe. But I'm enjoying the frisson of nervous energy,' I said. 'This is just like when

Bob Dylan went to find Woody Guthrie in Greystone Hospital.'

She raised her eyebrows again.

'Sort of,' I said.

It was a draughty, rattling train, on its way out to Blackpool. Shelley adjusted her hat in the dark window as we went through a tunnel. When we got to Macclesfield I said, 'Here we are then. Entertainment capital of the North.'

'Yeah,' she said. 'If you find men bopping each other on the head with pool cues up and down the high street entertaining. Which way to Babylon?'

I led the way up the hill. It was freezing so I walked fast. I needed Shelley to make sure I went through with this, to whatever end. And what I'd said was true; I was getting by on nervous energy. Perhaps I should have let Steven be. People should be allowed to disappear if they want to. I always wanted me and Tony to vanish. Vanish and not be asked after. Also, although it sounds crass, I wanted to show myself the worst, which is an innocent mistake, isn't it? I maintain that it is.

'So what will you say to him?' Shelley said.

'Oh, I'll just talk to him,' I said, 'I can talk to anyone, me.'

When we reached the end of his street I told Shelley to hold up a second.

'I've never been further than this before,' I said.

It was a quiet street of council semis. We walked up trying to make out the house numbers, which were hidden behind ladders and ivy and empty hanging baskets. Soon enough I spotted the place we were looking for. The front room was dark but I could see a light at the side so we walked down there. There was a row of ornaments on the kitchen windowsill behind a brightly patterned blind. I got the giggles and had to run down the path and back again. Shelley gave me a look. She flicked her spent cigarette into a grid and clapped her gloved hands together.

'Let's do this, sister,' she said.

I was glad she was with me.

I pressed the bell next to the frosted glass door, heard it chime inside. A security light had blinked on above us. I looked over at Shelley's face as she stood next to me and stared blankly ahead.

The girl who answered the door looked a little younger than us. But I think that was just because she was short and skinny. She was wearing jeans, a white shirt and a black, beaded cardigan. She had cropped brown hair and a pretty face. Steven's sister, it had to be. She looked just like him. She stood in the doorway in her bare feet, looking expectant, hugging herself. Past her, in their living room, I could see an old guy leaning back in his armchair to see who was calling. That room was lit by a fringed table lamp and the unsteady flare of the TV. He had thick, square glasses on and combed over hair and he was frowning behind a chuff of cigarette smoke.

'Hi,' I said, 'is Steven there please.'

I felt like I was eight years old, calling on someone to play out with me. Not that I'd ever done that, of course. Of course.

His sister stepped out on the ledge and pulled the frosted glass door to behind her. She balanced on the step in her bare feet, and periodically, while we talked, leant out and waved her hand under the Georgian-style security light to activate it. So we were lit up and then we were in the dark again, Shelley and I.

'He doesn't live here at the moment,' she said. 'Are you friends of his, or . . .'

'Yeah, sort of,' Shelley said, before I could answer, 'but we've not seen him in a long time. We saw Neil out the other night. He gave us this address.'

She rolled her eyes at the mention of his name.

'Oh, Neil,' she said. 'He's still hanging around, is he. Pissed I suppose?'

Shelley nodded and sucked air through her teeth.

'We didn't realise this was his family's house. We're really sorry,' she said.

His sister shrugged and smiled.

'No, don't worry about it. Steve was here a while ago but he's gone again. I can give you another address. Have you come far?'

'No, no,' I said. 'Just from Manchester.'

'I don't know why Neil would tell you to come here,' she said, then, 'I'll just get a pen, hang on.'

She went back inside and I heard her saying, It's all right, Dad, it's for me.

I mouthed *I didn't know* at Shelley, and shrugged my shoulders.

It's okay, she whispered.

Steven's sister came back with an address written on a yellow Post-it note. She handed it to me and I read it then folded it and put it in my wallet.

'That's where he'll be for the next few weeks,' she said, then bit her lip and said, 'You know he's in a pretty bad way.'

'Yeah,' we nodded, both of us, and apologised again, and thanked her and then left.

As we walked back down his road Shelley let out a long low whistle.

'She was dead nice, wasn't she? She should have told us to fuck right off.'

'Yes, perhaps. His sister, wasn't it?'

'Mmm . . . And was that his old man peering out at us?'

I laughed. 'No, his dad disappeared. His dad used to beat up his mum. That must be his step-dad.'

'She knew we weren't "old friends" you know,' Shelley said, making quotes in the air.

'Yeah, I realised that.'

'Where's our next port of call?' she said.

'Not today,' I said.

'Oh, okay . . .'

'But I'm going to go up to the university to see a band if you fancy it.'

Shelley nodded, then opened her bag and passed me another bottle. I downed it in two long swigs.

'Grim fucking place,' I said.

She nodded. 'Do you want to run down here,' I said. I was ambling along with my hands in my pockets. 'Because I'd quite like to run it.'

I took out my wallet and put it between my teeth so it wouldn't fall out of my pocket. I nodded at Shelley, took a breath and then started bombing it down the hill.

The thing about these All Stars is they have no cushioning, you really pound along when you run. The soles of your feet hurt from slamming on the pavement. It's good though. It's all right.

By the bottom of the hill my head was spinning from breathing in the night mist, which was rising fast. Shelley was kneeling down to tie her shoe. A likely story. I signalled to her that I was going up the embankment, and to wind her up I flashed my eyes and shouted, 'Going for a waz.'

I climbed up the scrub and picked my way through until I wasn't visible from the road, snapping the black bracken branches of the dead trees. It was freezing cold and I hopped from leg to leg, trying to warm myself up.

*

When we got back to town we went down to a private members club, just off King Street. I can get in because the bouncer used to work at our place. Every time I go there it's not so good as I remember. In my mind I see a wonderful Northern Gothic scene; the swirling red floral carpet, the nicotine-stained white walls; men with bubblegum tattoos, a gold chain-laden landlady and a tinsel curtain, shimmering, *floating*, behind a dance floor filled with couples who are, as an old man once leant over and said to me, *Married, but not to each other!* I'd widened my eyes at that and he'd chuckled.

The waitress brought me and Shelley a cocktail glass full of mixed nuts with our drinks and when she delivered the bill it was in a little leatherette wallet. There was a man in a pea-green tuxedo sitting at a small white organ. Shelley thought it was all great and went off to have a look round. Just after she left somebody tapped me on the shoulder. Vince.

I rolled my eyes and said, 'Hey there Vince.'

'You're looking lovely, as always,' he said, keeping his hand on my shoulder, to keep himself steady.

'Well thank you,' I said, and looked around in my seat for Shelley, 'but I can promise you I am rotten to the core.'

'Me too!' he said, delighted. 'Me too, sweet-heart.' He sat down with a sigh. 'What do you say. I'll give you my number and if you're ever feeling low call me up and I'll take you for dinner on Deansgate.'

Shelley came back then and rescued me, but for the next hour, every time our paths crossed going to and from the bar, Vince said, 'Dinner on Deansgate, Dinner on Deansgate.' I started ignoring him, and then, later on, he just said, quietly, 'I'm imagining you two in the shower . . .'

I said to Shelley, 'He's a real fucking prick, just one of these people who's been hanging round Manchester donkey's years. I guess time flies . . . when you're bloody miserable.'

The pianist had left his stool and was getting drunk at the bar. I found some change and went over to the jukebox, put on some silly old rock tunes: Starship, 'We Built This City On Rock And Roll'.

'I tried to leave the bar once, you know,' I said to Shelley. 'I applied for a job at a café-bar in Castlefield. Eighty pence more an hour and finished at seven every day. No more late nights. I must have been mad.' I swung my legs up and over the arm of the chair. 'The other bar staff were bitches. There was a middle-aged brat called Deborah who said to me, "It's full of bloody shoppers, in here, y'know, *Can I have a soup? Can I have a sandwich?*" Neat little trouser suit, false nails. Poor old Deborah. She hated her life. The other one was doing radiography at Salford and . . . I thought *Christ*. I ran away. And I'm ashamed to say I mean that completely literally.'

Shelley laughed. 'You're not one to keep things bottled up, are you?' she said.

I shrugged. I'm not sure if I am or I'm not.

Shelley looked very serious all of a sudden. 'Carmel,' she said, 'do you ever worry that you're going to end up like that woman who came in that time. The old lush. Because I do.' She shook her head. '*I get so scared.*'

It was an awkward question. I batted it off. 'No, no. No. These are just the wilderness years.'

'To be followed by . . .'

I shrugged. 'The Hollywood years, the smack years maybe, the draughts years . . . Come on,' I said, 'sup up, we don't want to be too late for this musical extravaganza.'

★

When we got to the university I spotted Arthur standing with some people and nodded hello as I went to the bar. He was showing his friends an old drum machine. Pulling it out of a white and blue Cash Generator carrier bag he grinned as he flicked the chunky orange switches, and different rhythms popped and pipped.

I couldn't see Margi or Gene anywhere, but I'd noticed Tony, on the other side of the room, with his sub-intelligent waitress friend. She was all dressed in red, with a red hat on her head. I pointed her out to Shelley.

'She looks like a fucking fire hydrant,' she said, blowing a stream of smoke out over my head.

'Can we go and piss against her, then?' I said. Very crude. I don't know where it came from.

Shelley said, 'Such obscene talk from such a pristine girl,' tutting, 'I know her. Well, I say know.

133

She used to come and buy decaff coffees off me for £2.80. The fool. And she never once looked me in the eye when I was serving her, but, then again, I never wanted her to frankly.'

I looked over again at Tony, tipping his bottle back between his teeth, his anorak zipped right up to the top as always. Felt odd. The truth is even my memories of Tony were going wrong. They faltered, they were being corrupted. Example: one time this summer we went down to Platt Fields, we were lying on the grass together, swigging ready mixed martini-lemonades from the Spar. We were talking daft, like people do, who are in love, or whatever. I'd put my forearm next to his and said, 'That's a Manchester tan.' Now I could recall the sour smell of sweat on his T-shirt, in his hair, but other details were confused. I couldn't get it right. In my mind's eye Tony got more and more vivid, looming in strange relief against the receding summer sky. But when I saw myself I really was bleaching out. In my memory the sun kept flashing through the branches. And hundreds of dandelion spores rained upwards, so slowly, all around us. I felt dizzy, suddenly. I asked for a swig of Shelley's water.

'I don't know, Shelley,' I said, and shook my

head. I felt awful, but I spoke with pomp. 'I can hear the shovel hitting the soil. I feel like Aschenbach in his deckchair. I feel like a waterlogged corpse. I can feel my life slipping through my hands like silk cord. That is to say, it's my birthday today, you know.'

Shelley raised her eyebrows and smiled, but she was looking straight ahead.

The backing tape had faded out and the lights were going down. There were whoops. There was a smattering of applause. Shelley put her fingers in her mouth and wolf-whistled as the band ambled on, heads down. There was Margi. She went and sat at the very front of the stage, cross-legged. She strapped on a bass guitar, visibly concentrating, and nervous probably. In the sweeping blue lights, with her black hair falling between her knees, she looked wonderful. Then the projections started to rush across all their faces: skyscraper windows, newsprint, car lights, rain? I couldn't tell.

Gene leant in to the mike. Squinted one eye up, 'This song's about a spider that gets caught in its own web.'

★

After the gig Shelley and I walked slowly back over to work.

It wasn't busy in there. Shelley ducked under the bar and told me to look away while her and Irene made me a 'special birthday drink'. She wiggled her eyebrows when she said that. So I turned and leant with my back to them, my elbows on the bar. I noticed that that old snooker star was in again, standing near the door with Bob. He looked worse than the last time, with his sandy hair grown too long and lying all greasy over the collar of his threadbare wool overcoat. His blueish bony hands held a half-drunk pint and his gaunt face was empty. He was talking, his eyes crinkling at the corners, and Bob was listening intently and nodding.

Shelley tapped me on the shoulders and when I turned around she passed me a formidable looking drink: three layers of colour in a pint pot, topped with whipped cream, cherries, umbrellas. Well they were parasols, really. Margi and I used to wish they'd make proper grey umbrellas for our drinks. I sucked some up through one of the straws. It tasted like coconut and vanilla and God knows what else.

'Classy,' I said. 'Cheers.'

Irene nodded and said she might be playing the piano when she'd closed up, any requests?

She twirled in her trainers and said, 'Ce soir, ce soir, nous dancerons sans pantalons.'

'You know I don't speak German,' I said. 'Just play . . . what I always ask you to play.'

She rolled her eyes. 'Maudlin anthems.'

Shelley and I sat down in a booth to share my ridiculous drink.

'Oh, he goes in Stanley's place as well,' Shelley said, pointing at the snooker guy with her straw. 'Work in any bar in Manchester long enough and he shows up. Him and Mark E. Smith.'

'What, together?' I said.

Irene called last orders and Bob started telling people to leave. At half past two the only people left were me and Shelley; Irene, cashing up, and Bob and the snooker player having an intense discussion by the door. Irene threw Bob a change bag: his wages. Bob eased a couple of notes out and dropped them in his new friend's hand. I leant back in my chair to listen in.

'Thank you, pal,' he said and nodded and shrugged, then he said, 'What are you doing Sunday?'

'Day off,' Bob said. 'Nothing planned.'

'Do you fancy a game of snooker, then?'

Suddenly, there was a rapping at the door. Bob went up to see who it was.

'Oh, hello there,' I heard him say. 'Long time no see.'

Tony followed Bob down the stairs, hands in his pockets and a grin on his face, so drunk he couldn't walk in a straight line. I could feel Irene giving me a look from behind the bar when he came in, but I didn't return it.

Tony stopped and smiled at me and then went over to the bar and sweet-talked Irene into giving him an after-hours drink. He pushed himself up on the bar, leaning over to give her a kiss on the cheek when she delivered his brandy and Coke, slamming the glass down on the bar. He shrugged off his anorak, leant on his skinny arms and looked over at me. I smiled and raised my eyebrows. He ambled over.

'Hey there, Tony,' I said, 'you old soak.'

He grinned, then crouched down by the table and put his hand on my waist and smiled at me. I felt strange. His grey eyes shone.

'So, do you know what very special day of the year it is?' I said.

He frowned for a moment then lifted his hands to his face and shook his head. His teeth were clicking, he chewed his words.

'It's not your birthday today, don't say that, Carmel, don't say that, I thought it was next week, I know when your birthday is . . . fuck, sorry, I'm so sorry.'

'S'all right,' I said.

He smiled at me. The tips of his front teeth thin and flaky from all his roll-ups. He smoothed his wet hair down in front of his ears, and smiled some more.

'Come outside, Carmel, where we can have a conversation,' he said, standing up. And I did. I did. I rose up, and went outside with him.

We were soaked through in seconds. We sat down together on the kerb and he put his drink down in the gutter. He leaned over and touched the top of my soaking wet head and brushed the hair out of my face. Then he slapped the flat of his hand onto the kerb, and shook his head, and said *Listen listen listen*. Then he was silent.

'Good birthday, yeah?' he said eventually.

'Yeah, I guess so . . . I mean, I can hear the shovel hitting the . . . I . . . yeah, as birthdays go.'

He laughed at me, Tony, said That's good to hear, and then he put his arm around me.

He took a deep breath. 'You won't talk to me anymore, Carmel . . . What attracted . . . attracted me to you in the first place was talking to you, and then you wouldn't talk to me and now you won't talk to me . . .'

He chewed his words and slapped his hands

139

on his knees, tilted his head back and laughed. I laughed too.

I said, 'Well, you finished with me Tony . . . for being unhappy . . . And I was happy, I really think I was.'

He shook his head and pressed his lips together.

'I didn't finish with you. You finished with me.'

I didn't know what he was talking about. He didn't either. He looked at me, grinning and rubbing the rain off his eyelashes. Tony. I thought, *Do you remember what passed between us, Tony?* He didn't. He didn't have a clue. Again he combed my wet hair back with his slim fingers and then I put my arms up around his neck. Easy as. We kissed for a while. I didn't close my eyes. I was drunk but he was wasted. He was gone.

He shook his head and looked away from me, saying, *I do love you, you know.* A cheap shot. He was fiddling with the fastener on my dress. We stood up and went back inside. I deliberately didn't look at Irene or Shelley. I stared at the floor as we walked past. Tony rattled the handle on the old kitchen door but it was locked. So we went into the disabled toilet together. Tony unbuttoned his jeans. Then he took my hands and put them one by one on the plastic rail on the back of the door. He lifted up my dress.

'Bend over,' he said.

And I did.

9

I got off the train in Macclesfield, alone. The windows of the huge pub opposite the station glowed a beautiful liquid yellow. Everything else was grey. I walked up the high street, found a newsagent's and bought a local A to Z and a half bottle of brandy to warm me up, then sat down on a low car park wall, sipping the brandy and examining the thin pages of the map opened out on my knees. Putting the bottle in my bag, I set off. The biting cold sharpened my senses. I inhaled icy air and dug my hands into the creases of my jeans pockets, all the while with a gathering feeling of walking to a destiny which had always belonged to me.

I found the house at the dead end of a long, uphill street whose houses became more run down and neglected the further I walked. I took the carefully folded Post-it note from my wallet and read the address which I already knew. The windows of the house were boarded up with splintering plywood; bottles and cans littered a weed-strangled garden. My heart beat in my throat as I knocked on the door. I had no idea what I was going to say. A skinny boy in a grey T-shirt and blue tracksuit bottoms answered the door and squinted at me.

'Hey there,' I said. 'I've come for Steven.'

The boy looked me up and down and sighed. He squinted at me some more. Turning to go back in, he said, 'He's in his room, you can just go up.'

I could hear voices and a badly tuned television set as I walked past the living room, and started to ascend the creaking stairs. There was a nasty, stale smell. There was lino nailed to the stairs. I heard two girls screaming at one another in the dark of one of the bedrooms on the first floor. I walked on, running my fingers along the smooth banister, on, on, on to the top, where a dim light flickered through an open door. I sat down on the top step and took a final, swift, scalding gulp of the brandy before standing up and entering softly.

Steven was curled up asleep on a camp bed, still fully dressed. There was no furniture save for the bed, though there were some candles, a tape recorder and a cardboard box full of tapes. I edged closer and as I looked at him I felt something welling inside me. At that moment I think the whole of my life stirred within me. Tiny beads of sweat stood out on his waxy skin, his unwashed hair was stuck to his face and his young bones jutted through thin, hopeless clothes. A blue T-shirt and black jeans. There was a thin duvet pulled up to his knees, the washed-out cover was patterned with bars of primary colours. It looked like something he'd had since he was a child, although I'm sure it wasn't.

I put my bag down and knelt by the bed. I saw his eyes were ringed with dark, bruised circles, and his lips were pale and scabbed; he was breathing, jerkily, through his mouth.

'Jesus, what have you done,' I whispered, 'look what you've done.'

I sat on the edge of the bed and slipped off my shoes. Then, carefully, I lay down in front of him and pulled his frail arm around me, holding onto his gentle, cold hand, and closing my eyes, in his small room, lit only by the dancing, dying flames of two church candles which stood on the floor by the bed with an ashtray, and a notepad.

*

The next morning I watched the pale sun rise over the chimney stacks from my corner seat on a dank, empty train back to Manchester. I had the prayer book Mackie had given me in my bag. I read the page he'd written on: *I acknowledge one Baptism for the remission of sins. And I look for the Resurrection of the dead. And the life of the world to come.*

Those words meant something to me. I read them again and again.

I bought an expensive coffee from a cart in Piccadilly Station and took too hot slugs of it as I walked down the approach amongst all the drones; the clip-clopping women and the men springing their umbrellas officiously. I'd arranged to meet Irene in the bar of the Palace Hotel at twelve o'clock. In the meantime I had a lot of thinking to do.

★

At the hotel, I felt revolted by the dull gold wrought in the arthritic chandeliers, the yellow light bulbs, the slab marble floors, the scuffed red walls, the yellow nets, the thickly glossed skirting. I felt the rattling trolleys, the running baths, the congress upstairs as a weight pressing down on me.

The barman had a moustache and wore a dicky bow. I didn't buy a drink. I saw Irene sitting upright on the edge of a stiff looking chintz armchair, way over in a corner, holding a huge globular cognac glass in her right hand, slowly swirling around the quarter inch of burnt gold. She was wearing the same clothes as the last time I'd seen her: big, dirty, painter's jeans and a hip, elaborately zipped long-sleeved black top. Her short red hair was pulled into a low, stubby pony-tail. I walked over and sat down opposite her.

'Let's go down to the canal,' was all I said.

She didn't even look up. 'What, and throw ourselves in?'

I sat down and started pushing a beer mat around the table, then drew swirls with my finger in the small pools of dripped drink. Some creep at the bar sent me a vodka and Coke over but I poured it straight into an ashtray without looking at him at all.

We left. Irene went into the Spar on Oxford Road and bought a bottle of Jack Daniel's, a big bottle of Coke and a slim jar of cocktail cher-ries. I waited outside. Irene came out as a train stopped on the bridge. We walked down Whitworth Street and she swung the carrier bag listlessly and kicked her small feet into the black puddles. This is what they're calling the post-industrial landscape. I think it's just worn out. The sky pressed down like iron.

We didn't talk. At the end of Deansgate we edged down a path of sharp red gravel stuck in frozen mud, and sat on the solitary bench, facing the canal. The wood was dark and icy cold with rain from the night before. We both sat with our legs pulled up and crossed. I stuck a finger through the various holes in my All Stars while Irene spun the lids off the two bottles and took a swig of each. She passed them onto me and I did the same. I ran my tongue over my chapped lips and scraped it across my chattering teeth, which felt furry from all last night's brandy. The ulcers were stinging on the roof of my mouth. Irene opened the jar of cherries, pulling her sleeve over her hand for more grip. She scooped out three with her fingers, ate one and dropped the others into my hand. For a long time we sat in silence. Drinking and shuddering off the cold. Then I looked up and saw a familiar figure hunching over the silhouetted bridge.

'Hey,' said Irene, smiling, 'there's Kevin in a trilby. Where's that reprobate off to?'

I yawned. 'He must be on a case.'

She called out to him and he looked up and tipped his hat to us. He seemed to want to say something. He looked down at his shoes and then up again. Then he cupped his hand around his mouth and shouted over,

'Wait until spring, Bandini!'

I smiled then shivered. Always the clichés with

Kevin. I pulled my hat further down over my ears and dug my sticky hands deep into my jacket pockets, which were full of dust and crumpled bus tickets. I closed my eyes and listened to the slow tug-tide of my breath.

'I want to move to Cornwall, Irene,' I said. 'Mackie goes there every year. He's told me all about it. It's a whole different life down there. There's different . . . flora and fauna and the children . . . are like pixies . . . I really think I should go there sometime soon.'

She nodded and stared ahead. Then we both started laughing.

*

This summer, there were five whole weeks without any rain at all, and on those long, pale afternoons I would use my whole body weight to push the window in my bedroom right up, so I could climb out, and sit out, with my bare feet dangling and the curtains floating behind me. I would press my palms onto the burning hot windowsill. And look out at the hazy blue sky over the zigzag of rooftops, imagining the atmosphere thinning to ether, to nothing. And then close my eyes and see all the colours. You know, the sun *really does kiss you*. He came out there with me once: jeans rolled up to his knees; tapping his ash into the gutter. And he told me about where he was from. And he said he was leaving Manchester someday to go back there.

'And you could sing to the sea,' I said.

'Yeah,' he grinned, 'and the sea could sing back.'

I think about that a lot. A place in the sun. An answering call.

29/8/03